A DOLLAR FROM THE STAGE

Young saddle-tramp Len Finch wasn't looking for much out of life — just a new shirt and a chance to work with cattle. What he found instead was a scene of death and a dollar stake in an unknown future. The pay-off was savage as he stumbled into a web of murder, lawlessness, intrigue and evil ambition. In the end, he put his life on the line for the folks that he cared about.

Books by Bill Morrison
in the Linford Western Library:

THE WOODEN GUN

F MORRISON

A dollar from the Stage

LARGE PRINT   £7.99

L 5/9

BILL MORRISON

A DOLLAR
FROM THE
STAGE

Complete and Unabridged

LINFORD
Leicester

First published in Great Britain in 1994 by
Robert Hale Limited
London

First Linford Edition
published 1997
by arrangement with
Robert Hale Limited
London

British Library CIP Data

Morrison, Bill
    A dollar from the stage.—Large print ed.—
Linford western library
    1. English fiction—20th century
    2. Large type books
    I. Title
    823.9'14 [F]

    ISBN 0–7089–5047–7

Published by
F. A. Thorpe (Publishing) Ltd.
Anstey, Leicestershire

Set by Words & Graphics Ltd.
Anstey, Leicestershire
Printed and bound in Great Britain by
T. J. Press (Padstow) Ltd., Padstow, Cornwall

This book is printed on acid-free paper

1

LEN FINCH caught sight of the stagecoach as his weary cow-pony climbed slowly to the crest of a little rise in the trail and the rolling grasslands opened out before him and swept off into the distance to merge with the heat-hazed brown of low hills.

He allowed his mount to draw to a halt and took off his hat to wipe the sweat from inside the brim. The heat struck hard through the straggling mass of his sandy hair and began to burn anew the blistered redness of his neck. His hand moved to refresh himself from the canteen at his saddle until he remembered that he had emptied the last few drops of water on to his parched tongue some hours before. The pebble he carried in his mouth in an attempt to induce saliva to alleviate his thirst moved from one side to the other as his youthful features took on an expression of puzzled interest.

The stage was still a long way off and appeared only as a tiny square of black in the sea of green and brown. He was a little surprised to see it and found himself wondering, in the vague way which had become characteristic of him over recent weeks, why it had stopped. He had known by its tracks on the trail and the broken grasses of its passage that it was up ahead of him somewhere, but he had believed that it was at least half a day in advance of himself and had not expected to see it at all, unless he should happen to catch up with it at the next township if it stayed there long enough to rest up or to change horses.

"Must be havin' wheel trouble or a hoss castin' a shoe . . . "

His voice trailed off and he scowled in irritation as he found himself speaking aloud to nobody but himself. It was a habit he knew himself to be falling into and one that he associated with old folks who were beginning to lose their wits through the ravages of age and the loneliness which so often accompanies it. He recognized that the loneliness of the trail was starting to get to him, too, and it worried him to think that he might be getting to be like Old Man Murphy who had owned the farm just over the river from the little cabin in which Len had been born and brought up and who talked to himself all day and half the night too, much to the amusement of his neighbours.

Len allowed his attention to slip away from the stage but at the same time deliberately veered his memory from those early years of his childhood which generally brought some feeling of sadness or regret along with them and which he thought he would do better to think of as seldom as possible.

The pony was breathing hard and suffering badly from the heat of the noonday sun. Len stroked its scrawny neck and flicked flies from the untidy mane. The pony was a mess, old and beat-up and just about finished, and he had bought it for the price of its carcase just as it was on its way to the knacker's yard. He had reckoned that it still had a little bit of time left in it, if it wasn't pushed too hard, and it was all he could afford by way of a horse for himself after he had been paid off from Taylor's place, where he had worked for a year or two as a cowhand, and where he would still have been if that calf hadn't broken its leg and he hadn't been blamed for it. He wasn't too sure even yet if he had really been at fault in the way he had used his rope or whether maybe he had just been unlucky, but the result had been the same anyhow and he had set out to look for other work in the same line but so far with no success.

Part of the trouble in finding the right kind of work had been the kind of country he had been travelling through. He had known straight off that it would be a waste of time trying any of the

ranches near-hand Taylor's p
Taylor was the kind of ma
liked to spread stories arou...
would have made Len's mistake — if
it was a mistake — seem worse than
it was and would, no doubt, have
invented a few others to go along
with it. For that reason, Len had
decided to move north, a long way
from the source of his troubles, but
had found the cow country to be
falling away behind him and a region
of small farmsteads, not unlike the
one he had been born on himself,
taking the place of rolling pasture,
and pigs and chickens replacing herds
of cattle. The change had not brought
him any satisfaction but, as he was
in no position to be choosy, he had
taken the only kind of work available,
and had shovelled manure and fed
livestock, driven a ploughing team of
mules through fields for days on end,
cut wood and mended fences and
had done all the other work of the
farm without complaint and for low

y until he could stand it no more and had set off again on his travels one early dawn when the day looked promising and he had some carefully saved dollars sewn into his pants.

A movement of the pony under him aroused his mind from its reverie and he slid from the saddle and sat down in the long dry grass partly in the shade of the animal. He did so with no idea of gaining respite for himself but solely because he wished to relieve his mount for a few moments from the burden of carrying him. In spite of the experiences of his young life, which had been less than fortunate, he had never taken on that defensive garb of selfishness and indifference to suffering which other young men in his situation might have assumed. There remained a kindliness in his nature which could not ignore the tiredness of his ageing pony and he longed for shade and water as much for its sake as for his own.

He slipped a grass stalk between his lips and chewed on it as he reflected

once again on his position. H   d
been on the trail for about three
since he left that last farm in the
coolness of the dawn, and now he
and his mount were both getting tired.
How far he could expect the pony to
carry him when it was so old and
half-starved was anybody's guess, and
he was running short of money and
had no prospect of getting any more
in the immediate future. He had, of
course, been as careful as he could in
the management of his limited funds,
but he had to eat and the animal had
to have corn from time to time and so
his little bundle of notes and coins had
gradually dwindled. For the first night
on his journey he had stayed in the
upstairs room of a saloon in a little
town he had come to and had paid
fifteen cents for the privilege, but he
had been kept awake all night by the
fellers downstairs who were having a
card-game and then a rough-house,
and even when the saloonkeeper and
his henchmen had herded the whole

unch of them out into the street they had gone on fighting all night. There hadn't been any shooting but one feller was still lying on the sidewalk in the morning, with his head all bloody and not looking too good, although the saloon-keeper had come out and thrown a bucket of water over him. After that disturbed night, Len had decided that it didn't make any sense to pay fifteen cents just to be kept from sleeping, so from then on he had slept under the stars and, as it was still the hot time of year, he had rested just fine and always had his fifteen cents in his pocket every morning to make him feel even better.

Even at that, his funds were running low and the only good news he had heard lately was when a feller driving a couple of mules had told him that there was a cattle-ranch not more than about twenty or thirty miles further up to the north-west and once he was on the stage-trail he could hardly miss it. That had been about forty miles back, so Len was beginning to wonder if the feller knew what he was talking about or if he, himself, had somehow got on to the wrong trail. One thing, though, the country was looking like cattle country and the sight of it was, in itself, a boost to his morale.

He stood up stiffly, feeling his joints ache from too many days in the saddle, and mounted up, full of the urge to get on his way and well aware that time spent motionless under the broiling sun was time badly spent and only marginally more restful to the pony than the slow walk which had become its normal pace of late.

As he moved forward, he caught sight once again of the stage and noted, with only slight interest, that it had not yet moved. His mind was busying itself with his own problems, however, and as the trail dipped down, and the little square of black slipped from view, it went also from his consciousness.

That mule-driver had told him as

much as he knew about the cattle-ranch. He had said it was pretty close to a little township called Barker's Fork, which was a place where plenty of beef was driven through on its way from ranches out west to the railhead away up to the north-east. He thought that the ranch was a big spread and was named Ranch Maria Theresa and was owned by some feller called Russe. That was all he could say about it because he had never seen it, but he knew that it was an important place judging by the way the townsfolk spoke about it.

Len had taken good careful mental note of these details as he was determined to try to find work there. Maria Theresa sounded kind of Mexican to him, though, and he wondered what it was doing so far north, but he couldn't afford to be particular about it and if he had to work for some Mexican feller he would just have to do it. He had made up his mind, just the same, that there was no way that he would ever wear a sombrero — this beat-up old hat he was wearing would do just fine — and he was going to stay a white man, though he wasn't too sure if Mexicans were white or what they were; but anyhow, he would just see what things were like when he got there and if he didn't like it and they expected him to grow a big moustache and wear a fancy waistcoat then he would just stay long enough to earn a few dollars and then he would move on.

Nevertheless, he hoped that it would be a good place and that he could get back to working with cattle and get friendly with some fellers like himself and be able to shake off the feeling of loneliness and aimlessness which had been dogging him for such a long time.

He wasn't quite sure how long he had had this empty feeling deep inside him. It was something that he wasn't aware of all the time, but every now and then, when he was too much on his own and had too much time to think, it seemed that a deep, lifeless cavern yawned open somewhere within him and that maybe it dated right back to the day when he had come back into the house to find his mother dead on the floor — or perhaps it had started even before then when his brother and his sisters had gone down with the same fever which had worked its way mercilessly through the family, somehow managing to miss him and leave him as a small, almost helpless survivor in the midst of the carnage.

But, what the hell, that was all a long time ago. He was a man now and had been ever since he knocked Abe Gummer's legs from under him and punched his head for calling him an orphan just after his ma's funeral, although he had often thought afterwards that maybe Abe hadn't meant anything by it — but it had seemed a bad thing to say at the time.

The trail was rising slowly again over the undulating grassland and by degrees the country ahead came again into view. This time the stage was much closer and he stopped and stared at it for long moments. He realized that he had expected to see some sign of movement — a man working with a wheel or handling a horse, people walking about, gesticulating in their annoyance, maddened by the long delay in the heat. But there was nothing like that. There was only stillness and silence and a buzzard circling high under the sun.

He pushed on a little faster, managing to urge the old pony into an awkward trot for a short distance until it gave up the effort and resorted to its ponderous but safer walk. And he recognized, a little to his surprise, that this more cautious approach suited his own mood too. His every instinct told him that there was something very wrong up ahead and because he had in him that deep-rooted awareness of danger that affects even the youth of the West, he was content to go forward slowly, his eyes and ears alert, his body tense in expectation of what he might find — or what might find him.

Now the stagecoach was fully in view, set at an angle to his line of vision, so that he could see part of its side as well as the rear. It seemed to him that one of the doors had swung open and a bundle of rags hung out from it. There was another mounded shape up on top near the front where he reckoned the driving-seat should be. Beyond that he could make out a mingled mass of grey and brown which could only be the team, still standing there waiting for orders that did not come.

As he came nearer, it became more and more obvious that the bundle of rags in the doorway was a corpse and that the lump on the driver's seat was probably another one. The realization made him gulp sorely in the dryness of his throat and one hand gripped the reins tightly while his other crept to the butt of the ancient hand-gun which hung from his belt. The gun was rusted and useless. He had picked it up for a few cents in a blacksmith's yard, partly because it had a good enough holster which he hoped one day to fill with an efficient weapon, and partly because he believed that it could be a useful bluff if he met some roughneck on the trail. Another reason, which he had to admit to himself with some amusement, was that it gave him a false confidence and he felt its useless weight as a comfort at his side.

He drew the gun with a start as the pony gave a little whinny and shied nervously at something that lay half hidden in the long grass and which the animal had almost trodden on. It was the body of a man, a big feller too, broad and strong and with a big moustache and rugged features, who looked as if he ought to have been able to take care of himself; but now he lay on his back, eyes staring blindly into the sun. He was stiff and cold-looking and had a gaping bloody hole in the side of his head and another in his chest. Whoever had shot him had made a determined job of it and it looked as if he had been shot down from the coach when it had been travelling, to judge by the queer way in which his left arm and leg were twisted under him.

Len had not seen many corpses before. The only one that sprang to mind was that of a cowpuncher whose horse had reared in front of stampeding cattle, and he had had his neck broken probably even before the cattle had trampled over him. He had been in a real mess too. The others he remembered, his family, well, they were in altogether a different category and belonged to a different era. The sight of this slaughtered human being filled him with horror, and he circled the pony around and then approached the scene of death with slow dread.

He stopped a little way off to survey the coach and its surroundings. All around the grass had been beaten flat as if horsemen had been riding up and down and to and fro across it. The stage stood sharply angled as if it had come to a sudden wild and dangerous stop, with the buckboard twisted to one side as if caught in a sharp turn. As he had seen from the distance, the door was wide open and beginning to swing slightly in the warm breeze that he could feel rising now from the west. The bundle of rags was, sure enough, a dead man, but he realized that he had done this one less than justice by the comparison because he was just about the best-dressed man he had ever seen and managing to look, even in death, smart and rich and prosperous.

The body lay head down out through the doorway, shoulders and face in the grass, legs still sprawling inside the coach. His hat lay nearby, jet black, shining and made of the most expensive felt from the East. The coat he wore was of the same colour and trimmed around the collar with silk, but had fallen open in the struggle with death to show an expanse of pure white shirt. On one finger there was a gold ring and there was the glint of a cuff-link at his wrist. To Len he looked like some rich businessman from the city except that the handsome lightly-moustached features were as deeply tanned as any cowpoke's and the hand with the gold ring looked strong and roughened. He looked like a man of about forty years old. The wounds he had received could not be seen but the grass beneath his chest had stained brown with drying blood.

Len sat in the saddle and stared for a long time and then he dismounted and took a few faltering, nervous steps towards the stage, not really knowing what he intended to do but feeling that some action on his part was necessary, however futile a gesture it turned out to be.

He looked past the expensive boots and into the interior of the coach and drew back with a little gasp as he saw another body inside. What made this seem more shocking was that it was obviously that of a woman. She lay crouched in a corner, a bullet-hole in her head and her grey travelling-clothes smeared in blood. His first thought was that this must be the rich feller's wife but then he saw that she was old and her clothes were plain and homespun. Whoever she was, he guessed that she had not been related to the man in the expensive clothes, but she had shared in the same fate, whatever the reason for that might have been.

Len moved on to the front of the stage and saw that the driver, grey-bearded and with his old dead face contorted into new lines of agony, was still seated on the buckboard, knees bent up as if to protect his belly from the bullets that had ripped it open, hands clasped over the gaping wound. In front stood the team heads drooping, suffering in the heat, ears and tails twitching fitfully against the tormenting flies.

Len stepped back a few paces, feeling

shocked and nauseated. He went to his pony as if to remount and then turned back and gaped again at the dead driver, the corpse in the doorway, the white face of the woman inside the darkened coach. He bent forward as though to throw up but could not do so on an empty and dry stomach. He took off his hat, ran his fingers through his hair and then jammed his hat back on again. He looked around wildly at the deserted landscape as if searching for a way of escape.

"Jeez, what's all this? What the blazes has been goin' on here? What the hell did this?"

His voice arose in a near shout of amazement and concern, almost as if he expected the distant hills to provide him with an answer. The lead horse of the team was startled by the sudden noise which broke the stillness of the long day. It raised its head and took a pace forward. The rest of the team moved to follow. The wheels of the stage made a half turn and the door flapped and then banged. The well-dressed corpse slid further to the ground and then remained still as the movement stopped.

"Jeez," whispered Len once more.

He had just noticed something that he would never have expected even in this scene of surprises that seemed to be stretching his credulity to the limits so that he was not sure if he was awake or had fallen into a bad dream while asleep in the sun. In the side of the stage, half hidden by the swinging door, there was an arrow, stuck in at about the height of a man's head. To Len it looked long and heavy for an arrow and it was fletched with white feathers and there hung from it a flash of white cloth like a little streamer. He stared at it in amazement for a moment and then made his way to the back of the coach where he remembered that something had caught his eye as he had ridden up with most of his attention fixed upon the bundle of rags in the door. Sure enough, it was another arrow, this one with striped feathers and much lighter in appearance than the first. And there was another arrow lying nearby in the grass just as if it too had been stuck into the side of the stage but had fallen out.

Len stood for what seemed a long time, looking about at the scene: the coach, the corpses, the silent team, the arrows . . . Indians? How could it be Indians? As far as Len was aware there had been no trouble from hostile Indians anywhere around the territory for years. Most of the Indian population that remained after the wars with the whites were now confined to reservations, although he had heard, from time to time, of outbreaks of trouble further to the west. He, himself, had rarely seen an Indian, apart from the tame ones who sometimes worked around the farms, and to find himself standing now at the scene of a redskin massacre seemed like something left over from his childhood imagination rather than adult reality.

He walked past the coach again, this time turning away his eyes from the sight of the woman inside, and stared once more at the horses. They were fine strong animals, weak and distressed now from their hours in the sun, but every one a valuable beast and not one injured or harmed in any way by the violence which had raged around them. He shook his head, disbelief rising inside him, and then bent to pick up an object which his foot had felt in the grass. It was a moccasin, made of buckskin, dry and old-looking but lying there just as if it had fallen from some mounted warrior's foot in the excitement of the battle.

The battle? What kind of a battle had it been? Had the whites been able to put up a good fight? If so then the Indians had carried away their dead and wounded, which was not unlikely. To Len, inexperienced in such matters as he was, it seemed to have been a quick, one-sided kind of conflict. There were no bullet-holes that he could see in the coach itself, none of the horses had been brought down. He had the impression that the feller in the door had made a sudden leap forward as if taken by surprise, though he could be wrong about that.

But how could Indians have made a successful ambush away out here, with no cover except the grass for miles around? The driver and the guard of the stage would have seen them coming from a long way off and surprise would have been impossible.

Len walked back to where the burly guard lay in the grass and studied him closely. He had almost certainly been shot off the stage when it was travelling at its normal speed. Len guessed that he had taken the chest wound first and that had toppled him from his perch on the roof. The other bullet, the one in the head, might have come a little later, just to make sure.

And that, it looked to Len, was the strange part. They had all been shot dead in a way that was meant to put paid to them once and for all and without much time being wasted. Even the old woman in the stage had taken a quick bullet before she could get out of her seat. Where was the mutilation, the scalping, the general messing-up that he had heard Indians went in for? Old Man Murphy, who had tangled with Indians in the old days, always said that they mutilated their enemies, just out of spite, so that they would be ugly and deformed when they went into the next world, which was a pretty nasty idea; but Len was ready to believe that they did just that, because Old Murphy, for all his talking to himself and all his crankiness, still knew a thing or two.

He went back to his pony and stood with his hand on the bridle as if about to ride off but still somehow unsure of what he should do. He would have to ride on to the next town or the next farm or wherever else he could find some people and let them know what he had seen. Hanging about here any longer was a waste of time and if anything was going to be done to get the polecats who had done this then the sooner the law got on to it the better.

He mounted up and urged his pony into movement. The beast gave a little snicker of irritation and the lead horse of the team again pricked up his ears and this time pulled forward two or three yards. The door of the stage banged wildly and the corpse in the black coat rolled out on to the ground. Len looked back and now saw that the man lay face upwards, his shirt front a mass of red. From under his armpit there protruded an empty holster and Len drew to a halt as he realized that he had seen no guns lying anywhere around. The guard could have dropped his rifle into the long grass as he fell from the stage so that it would be hard to find, but the driver would almost certainly have carried one, too, and the well-dressed feller had been armed with a hand-gun of some kind which was now nowhere to be seen.

So the Indians had taken the firearms, as was natural, but what else had they taken? Why not the smart-jet black hat? Why not the lady's parasol, cheap-looking though it was by white standards? These were the kinds of things that Old Murphy had said that Indians took a delight in. And why was it that the driver still carried a knife in its sheath at his belt, and, most puzzling of all, why were all these fine horses, the prize booty of any Indian war-party, still left attached to the stage?

His eyes, searching for more clues, opened wide in surprise as he caught sight of something lying on the floor of the stage just where the rich feller's left boot had been. It was an envelope, buff-coloured and important-looking. Len dismounted and went forward with a slight hesitation that he would not have understood even if he had thought about it, and stretched his hand over the corpse to the coach floor. He picked up the letter with the feeling that he was stealing something from a coffin and held it respectfully by one corner as he examined it.

The first thing he noticed was that it contained an object of some slight weight which was round and hard like a silver dollar. He ran his fingers over this before turning the envelope around to read the writing on the other side. The handwriting was in black ink, with well-formed copperplate letters of the kind that Miss Trudy had spent many hours trying, with only moderate success, to teach Len and his classmates to master in that tiny, ill-lit schoolroom at Saffron Creek. Whoever had addressed the letter was a person of some education, a fact that made some impression on Len. He had always had a certain respect for education, mainly due to the emphasis placed upon its importance by the dedicated Miss Trudy, for whom he had a lasting and secret admiration.

He read the name and address slowly and with an expression of surprise spreading across his features, as it was intended for a Mr Kurt Russe, Maria Theresa Ranch, Near Barker's Fork, Montana . . .

Len stepped back and looked again at the dead man at his feet. Could this be Mr Russe, the owner of the Maria Theresa? He looked like a rich rancher, certainly, and it seemed likely that the letter had fallen out of his pocket when he had attempted to draw his gun, but why then was the envelope still sealed? Surely if it was his letter he would have read it on the long stagecoach journey, if not before! It seemed more likely that this man, whoever he was, had been carrying the letter to deliver to Mr Russe at the ranch.

Len placed the letter carefully upon the padded seat of the coach and then went to his pony and mounted up. He had not ridden many yards when he turned around and went back to pick up the letter and place it inside his waistcoat pocket. It seemed wrong to leave it there in the coach where it might blow out with the rising wind and become lost in the grass or where some saddle-tramp might come along in the next hour or two and find it. Since he had found it, it was up to him to take care of it. He could give it to the sheriff or somebody up in Barker's Fork or he might meet Mr Russe and deliver it to him personally.

The truth was, as he knew very well a moment later when he decided to be honest with himself, he saw this as a good opportunity of making himself known to Mr Russe. He saw himself riding up to the ranch-house to deliver the important letter, Mr Russe shaking hands with him, expressing his gratitude, some conversation and then the offer of work.

He found it hard to believe his luck. It just showed, as Miss Trudy was inclined to say, that it's an ill wind that doesn't blow anybody any good. It was too bad about what had happened. It was a terrible thing that these people had been murdered and it was going to cause a lot of trouble yet, but he could see himself gaining some advantage from it. That thought, however, pricked his conscience real hard; but however much he thought about it, he couldn't see that he was doing anything wrong. Somebody had to give that letter to its rightful owner, so why not him?

Even so, all the dead people lying back there in the grass and in the coach kept telling him that he had no right to feel the slightest bit pleased or uplifted about the way things were going and he knew that they were right.

The thought troubled him all the time that his old pony plodded along the trail in the general direction of Barker's Fork and it got him so downcast in his feelings that he hardly noticed at first that the land was falling away in front of him into a kind of valley. It was only when the glint of a river caught his attention that he sat up in the saddle and saw clumps of trees overhanging the water and felt the inviting coolness of the shade.

He realized fully then that he would soon be meeting up with people and that when he told them the news everything was going to change, because you can't tell folks something like that without having them look at you in a different way.

2

OLD SKIN sat on a hummock of grass near the bank of the river. The late afternoon sun darted here and there through gaps in the overhanging foliage and caught the surface of the water, creating patterns of dancing light. Overhead, songbirds were engaged in their evening chorus as if in anticipation of the coming of darkness.

There was a certain beauty and peace prevailing and yet Skin was not in good spirits and stared glumly towards the opposite bank with all the appearance of a man wrapped up deeply in his own troubles.

He had just finished consuming a trout which he had caught with some difficulty earlier in the day, a fact which had pleased him mightily at the time as he seldom had success in his fishing now that his arms were beginning to stiffen with old age and he found the capture of a fish with his bare hands a much more difficult task than it had been when he was young and nimble and expert.

He had enjoyed eating the trout after roasting it on a stick on his little fire but he had, unfortunately, bitten too hard on a rotten molar and the pain was irksome. He also had an ache in his old knees, which was the reason he was sitting on a grass hummock instead of cross-legged, Indian fashion. From time to time, he rubbed his aching joints, and, once in a while, he removed the lump of resin from his mouth to examine it, for no particular reason, before placing it carefully once again on his bad tooth. It was a remedy for toothache which his grandfather had used and therefore ought to be effective, although he was beginning to have to admit to himself that his frequent bouts of pain over recent months had generally run their course with or without the treatment.

The pains of his ageing body were not, however, the main reason for his mood. It had been a queer, disturbing kind of a day and his mind was in a turmoil of worry although he told himself that none of it had anything to do with him and that he would just forget about it.

Things had seemed all right in the early morning when he had crawled out of the tiny shack he had built for himself out of old planks and branches in the woods just below Martha Benn's place. The sun had promised a fine day and he had been feeling pretty fit. He had drunk hot coffee and smoked the last of his tobacco and had planned, at first, to go in to see Martha as he knew that she would want the chicken-coop cleaned out and there would be the sweeping of the yard and some weeding to be done in the vegetable patch. Then she would give him a share of whatever they were eating and a few cents for his work and he reckoned that he would still have time to walk into Barker's Fork to the grocery store and buy some more tobacco. The next day, he might go over to the Johnstone place and cut up wood, which was hard work, but he could earn enough from that to return again to the town, this time to the back door of O'Hara's saloon and get his tin mug filled with a mixture of water and whiskey which he could carry carefully back to his hut and sip throughout the evening.

In spite of these well-considered plans, everything had worked out quite differently. The trouble had started, he supposed, because he had been feeling too good, had slept better than usual and had just awakened from a pleasant dream about the buffalo and had seen the face of Little Bead Woman smiling as she sewed his moccasins and stirred the black kettle in the tepee.

It was that dream which had put him in the mood to walk downriver until he left the trees behind and then to climb the grass slopes to a high point from which he could look far over the open range to the south and west. It was a little journey he had made often enough before, usually when he was feeling lonely and depressed. On that high point he could close his eyes and feel the wind in his face and see, in his imagination, the buffalo herds and ride again with his brothers across the wind-swept prairies.

Today, however, he had gone for the opposite reason, because he was feeling good and it seemed that Little Bead Woman had invited him.

But he had not seen the buffalo or experienced that uplifting sense of freedom. Instead he had seen something that had aroused his suspicion and, when curiosity had drawn him nearer, he had seen things that he would have preferred not to see because it was bad medicine, white man's bad business, and his every instinct told him to keep his head down from the storm that he saw gathering over and the thunderbolts he could feel in the air.

So he had come back to the river and had resolved to say nothing and to do nothing, for an Indian who gets himself mixed up in the troubles of the white man is very likely to take the first bullet.

Nevertheless, he could not dismiss the matter from his mind all that easily because big trouble generally catches up with the innocent as well as the guilty, and there were some white folks that he did care about.

He sighed and drew his gnarled old fingers through the braids of his grey hair and then stood up stiffly and looked away back through the trees to where the sunlight still lit up the grassy banks. In spite of his years, his ears and eyes were still good and he heard and then saw a rider making his way along the narrow trail which followed the river at that stretch. He observed that the pony was going real slow in spite of the rider's efforts to urge it on a little faster. From the direction he had come, Skin knew that this white man had seen what he himself had come across earlier in the day.

Old Skin sat down once again on the hummock and looked over the water. He heard the sounds of the rider coming closer along the trail and then the sounds of him dismounting and leading the pony down through the trees. He stopped close by and Skin continued to stare at the river as he listened to the pony being tied to a branch so as to allow it to cool off before drinking. There was a silence, broken only by the heavy breathing of the pony and the lighter breath of the man.

"Hi!" The voice was a little hesitant as if unsure about awakening the old Indian from his apparent reverie.

Skin turned his head. The young feller looked hot and weary as if he had ridden a long way. His face, although still carrying much of the optimism of youth, was beginning to show some trace of the lines around the eyes and the mouth which come to men who spend their lives in the saddle.

"Hi!" replied Skin.

Len looked closely at the old Indian, wondering if he was the right person to talk to, but he had seen no other living person all day.

"I got real bad news."

What other kind is there, asked Skin, in his mind.

"Somethin' terrible's happened."

He's goin' to tell me about the stage, thought Skin.

"The stagecoach has been all shot up. They're all killed."

"That so?" grunted Skin.

"Looks as if it might be Injuns — arrows all over the place."

Yeah, Omaha, Cheyenne, Shoshone, reflected Skin, his mind twisting into a kind of sarcasm.

"And I found an Indian moccasin."

That was from the Lacota, remembered Skin. Queerest mixed-up war-party I ever heard of . . .

"Only they never did no scalpin' and the horses weren't took."

40

Kid's not so dumb, thought Skin.

Len studied the old Indian closely as if expecting an expert opinion.

"Injuns usually take the horses, don't they . . . and scalp? What do ya think?"

"Don't know," answered Skin.

"Injuns generally hack people up, don't they? Steal everythin' too?"

"Don't know."

"You're an Injun, ain't ya?"

"Yeah, Pawnee."

Len gazed in silence at the old Indian, taking in his world-weariness, his worn, cast-off white man's clothing. Then he turned and went down to the water and bathed his face and upper body and drank a little. After that, he brought the pony down carefully and allowed it to drink also but not too much. When he had finished he spoke again to the old Pawnee.

"This town, Barker's Fork, how far is it?"

"Bit less than an hour's ride — on a good horse," answered Skin, glancing at the pony.

"Critter's all tuckered out. Finished for today, anyhow."

"Yeah." Skin had come to the conclusion that the young feller wasn't too bad. It wouldn't do any harm to take him up to Martha's place and it wouldn't mean that he, himself, was getting mixed up in things since he was walking back that way in any case. "There's folks nearer hand than Barker's Fork. If you want to talk to them, I kin show ya."

They followed a twisting trail up through the trees, Len leading the pony, until they came to a place where the timber had been felled many years before and a broad field of ripening maize stretched out in front of them. Beyond that there was another field, this one fenced around, and on the other side of that they could see a small house of mixed stone and timber. Skin led the way, skirting the fields carefully so as not to crush down the maize or tread on the vegetables, and then struck on to a broader pathway which led directly to a gate just opposite the main door. There he stopped and motioned for Len to tie up the pony.

"Mrs Benn — Ma'am!" Skin's voice took on a note of mixed familiarity and respect.

A woman came out of the door and on to the porch with an alacrity which indicated that she had already observed their arrival. She was of smallish stature, thin and grey-haired. She wore a dress of faded blue and a clean white apron. Her eyes narrowed as she stared at Len.

"Well, Red, who's this you're bringing in?"

"Young feller just rode in."

Martha examined Len closely, noting his travel-stained clothes, his straggling hair, the gun at his hip, the worn-out nag at the fence.

"Saddle-tramp," she muttered under her breath, then, more loudly, "If he's lookin' for free lodgings, I guess he kin jest move on, Red."

She always called Skin 'Red'. One

day, in a mood for confidences, he had told her that his real name, when translated into English, came out as Redwing, and that it was only after he had got mixed up with the whites and the slaughter of the buffalo that he had been called Buffalo Skinner and, later on, Skin and a few other even less flattering terms. To her, 'Skin' sounded somehow coarse and insulting and maybe hurtful to the old man, so 'Red' it had been ever since.

Not that it really mattered to old Skin. He did not care what the whites called him because he held the name of his youth, Redwing, close to his heart as a secret symbol of a sacred past.

"Ma'am!" Len had removed his hat in a gesture of courtesy. "I ain't lookin' for lodgings. I've got real bad news. The stage has been ambushed. Everybody's killed."

There was a moment of silence. He thought he saw her hand tighten on the rail that ran around the porch.

"Well, if that's so, young feller, you'd

better come in and tell me some more. Hang up that gun on the fence."

They went inside to the main room of the house, plainly furnished and with an iron stove to one side. A bunch of wild flowers stood in the window. There was a Bible on the sideboard and a picture of a middle-aged man and woman on the wall. Martha sat down on one of the hickory chairs and signalled for her two guests to do the same.

"Let's hear what you have to say, young feller, and nothin' but the truth. What's your name, for a start?"

Len told her and then went on to describe how he had found the stage and the terrible scene of massacre he had witnessed. When he got to the end of his story, she remained silent for a few minutes before seeming to rouse herself.

"Seems to me that you'd better get into town and see the sheriff. His name's Holt — Sam Holt. Office is in the main street."

45

"That's what I was aiming to do but my pony can't go any further. It's fair worn out. I'd be quicker walkin'."

Martha studied him carefully. He looked honest enough and returned her stare with a candour that suggested he had nothing to hide, but she had lived too long and had been betrayed too often to consider letting this young stranger ride off on one of her few horses, possibly never to be seen again.

"I'll send Lee Sanger. He's doin' some day labouring for me in the upper meadow. You go and get him, Red. I'll make coffee."

When Skin returned with Lee Sanger, having plodded part of the way across the meadow and shouted the rest, they were joined by a young girl who seemed to have been working on some other part of the farm, unaware of the visitors. Len sat up and stared as she came into the room for she was dark-haired and pretty. She looked equally surprised to see him but then assumed an air of indifference.

"This here's my granddaughter, Emma. This is Mr Len Finch," said Martha. "Just come in with bad news. Stage's been ambushed."

Len arose clumsily to his feet, suddenly anxious to make a good impression, and saw the little smile which had begun to lighten up her face vanish as the last few words sank in.

"What, the stage?"

"Yes, young feller found them all dead. We're sendin' for the sheriff."

Martha repeated the story that Len had told her and then turned to Lee Sanger and asked him to take his horse into Barker's Fork and fetch Sam Holt. Sanger, middle-aged, surly and now tired after his day's work, seemed less than enthusiastic even in these pressing circumstances.

"You only got to ride a mile or two past your own place," snapped Martha. "And you're gettin' off with some of your work. There's still an hour of daylight left!"

They listened to Sanger riding off

while Martha poured coffee and then sat down at table. Len was acutely aware of his dirty clothes, the half-grown youthful stubble on his chin, and the odour of drying perspiration which hung about him. He felt like joining Skin, who had taken his coffee over to the stove, in order not to offend the ladies, both of whom seemed clean and fresh in spite of a busy day. He realized, however, that he could not move from the table without appearing impolite.

"Tell us about yourself, Mr Finch," demanded Martha, with an interested stare which increased his embarrassment.

Stumbling over his words, he outlined the history of his short life and watched a sympathetic light come into her eyes when he mentioned what had happened to his family. The girl listened with quiet attention and he was aware that the defensive attitude she had displayed at their first few seconds of meeting had now evaporated.

"So you're lookin' for work right

now," commented Martha when he had finished. "You'll know somethin' about farming?"

"Yeah, that I do, ma'am, but I was hopin' to get back to cattle, if I can. Somebody told me 'bout this ranch near here, the Maria Theresa."

He watched their backs stiffen at the mention of the name. An icy gleam came into Martha's eyes. The girl frowned and looked at the wall. He faltered on, aware of the tension rising in the room.

"The thing is, it's what I really like doin'."

The cold silence continued. Skin looked gloomily into the stove.

"I thought I might get work at that ranch, and . . . " he tugged the letter out of his pocket as if it would somehow lend support to his argument " . . . I found this letter at the stage. It was jest lyin' there inside. It's addressed to Mr Russe, Mr Kurt Russe, Maria Theresa . . . " Both sets of female lips tightened and he hesitated again, feeling that he had put his feet in a cowpat. "I guess I'd better see that he gets it."

"Yes, I should think so, young man." Martha sounded dignified and aloof. "If that letter's for Mr Kurt Russe, then no doubt he should get it."

"I think there's money in it. Feels like a silver dollar. Maybe somebody payin' back somethin' owed."

"Wouldn't have thought there were any more folks left in that situation," broke in Emma, her voice full of sarcasm. "Seems to me . . . "

"Now, now, girl, remember Mr Finch is a stranger here."

"Ain't likely to forget," pouted Emma.

Len shoved the letter back into his pocket, feeling that he had made too much of it.

"Well, anyhow, I need to git myself working as a cowpuncher." He was starting to feel rattled and irritated, as if he had made a real fool of himself, though with no idea how he had achieved it. "So, I guess I'll see if they need any hands there. I heard it was a pretty big spread."

"The biggest, there is," agreed Martha.

"The only one there is," added Emma, "now that the other three have gone."

"Thet so?" breathed Len, greatly interested.

"Great big place," went on Emma. "Stretches for miles and miles. Nobody can ever find the end of it. Feller like you could get lost up there, no trouble." Her tone seemed to imply that she personally would be perfectly pleased if he did exactly that. "Could just disappear like a bug in the desert."

"Don't let's have any of your sass, girl," Martha snapped. "Mind your tongue and give Mr Finch some more coffee."

She began to talk again about Saffron Creek, asking him more questions as if she was really interested. He knew that she was just trying to make him feel more comfortable after his obvious embarrassment. He responded by expressing admiration for the farm and comparing it favourably with a good many others he had seen and worked on. The polite conversation went on for some time before she suggested that he ought to attend to his pony.

"Here, Red, take our young friend down to the south paddock. The pony can stay there meanwhile. And get some feed for it too. Poor critter looks half-starved; no fault, I'm sure, of yours, Mr Finch. That can happen on a long trail. Looks like you'll be stayin' the night, so make yourself at home in the barn. Sorry I can't do better for you right now but I wasn't expecting visitors."

The pony was safely installed in the paddock on fresh grass and its immediate hunger satisfied with a bag of corn. In the gathering darkness, Skin led the way around to the barn, where there was clean hay and the prospect of Len having a more comfortable night than he had spent for some time. They were on the point of parting company when they heard hoofbeats and then a man's voice raised at the front of the house.

"Mrs Benn! Ma'am! Kin we speak to you? Sorry 'bout the time o' night, an' all."

The door was opened. The gleam of a lamp shone out around the corner of the building.

"Sorry to disturb you, ma'am, but Sheriff Holt says we was to bring down the feller who found the stage. The rest of the posse is waitin' down on the trail. Hope the feller's still here, ain't he?"

Len strapped on his gunbelt once again, shut the barn door and walked around to the front of the house.

"Who is that there?" Martha was asking, her head and shoulders thrusting into view at the doorpost. "Is that Bret Williams?"

"Yeah, it's me, ma'am, an' that's Beebo Kelly at the gate."

"Well, you can just tell Beebo Kelly

to get off my property!" Her voice rose in sudden anger. "I ain't havin' any Kellys on my land! Get him off!"

"All right! No need for ya to be screechin' like a wildcat." Beebo Kelly sounded exasperated and angry. "Jest doin' my duty. I'm a sworn-in deputy an' don't you forget it, Martha Benn!"

"Some deputy! Don't know what Sam Holt's thinkin' about . . ."

"OK, let's cool it," interrupted Williams. "This looks like the feller, here, ain't it?"

"That's me," agreed Len, grimacing as he guessed what was to come.

"Sheriff says thet he wants you with us when we's searchin' for the stage. You'd better come along."

"Ain't got a hoss."

"So we heard tell but we brought a spare so let's git goin'. Whole bunch of us is sick o' this already but Holt ain't gonna wait 'til mornin'."

He turned his mount around and followed Beebo Kelly down the path. Len trudged after the horses, trying to shake off the exhaustion of the day. Old Skin was shuffling along beside him. They were still about fifty yards from the spot where a group of horsemen could be seen dimly against the night sky when Skin suddenly staggered and fell, clutching at Len's gunbelt as he went. They fell over in a heap and Len crunched his elbow into the gravels of the path. Skin was rolling about and groaning, hanging on to Len's clothing as he writhed in pain. They disentangled themselves and Len struggled to his feet while Skin sat on the ground, rubbing his knees.

"What the hell's goin' on? Who's thet?" shouted Bret Williams.

"Sounds like thet drunk old bastard of an Injun!" yelled Kelly. "What the hell's he doin' around here at this time o' night?"

"You all right?" Len bent down, peering into the twisting face of the old man.

"Damn knees givin' out again. Sore

like the great bear biting! Sorry. Damn old knees . . . "

"Come on!" Williams was slumped in the saddle, his entire being consumed with a weary impatience. "We ain't got all night. Least I goddamn well hope we haven't."

Len moved on, aware of Skin rising slowly to follow. He stopped and looked back. Skin motioned him onwards.

"Don't worry about me. I'm just crawlin' back to the shack. Thanks, Mr Finch. See you around."

Len wished, at that moment, that he had a shack to crawl back to himself, but there was no escape from Sheriff Holt and the posse and he soon found himself mounted on a roan and riding alongside Bret Williams. They had passed through the woods and had made several miles over the open grasslands when Holt dropped back a little to exchange a few words.

"Where are you from, Finch?" Holt sounded unfriendly, suspicious.

"Saffron Creek." Len curbed his

resentment with difficulty.

"Never heard of it." The sheriff sounded as if Len had damned himself by admitting that he came from a place that nobody in the world had ever heard of. "I'll be wantin' a clear written statement from you 'bout all of this later. Right now, I want you ridin' with me at the head of the column. And I'll take thet gun."

"You puttin' me under arrest or somethin'?"

"Nope. Jest my rules, son."

The moon had come up and was casting an eerie light over the bleak landscape when they came in sight of the stagecoach. Holt led the way cautiously towards it and then signalled for his men to fan out as if to haze out any remaining Indians who might be still crouching in the grass. All was silent, however, apart from the team of horses which began to fidget and whinny in excitement as the horsemen approached.

Lamps were lit and Len saw again

the faces of the dead. The posse dismounted and searched everywhere around the area. The arrows were gathered in and Len pointed out the moccasin in the grass. Then Holt ordered that the corpses should be lifted and placed inside the coach and a man clambered up to drive the team. The horses, distressed still by hunger and thirst, but cool now in the night air, were pleased to get on the move.

The column dragged slowly back along the trail like a funeral procession which had somehow lost its way in the darkness. The team driver seemed to feel that his cargo of the dead made any suggestion of haste somehow unseemly and moved at an even slower pace than the moonlight made necessary. The sheriff made no objection and the journey through the night became, to Len, like a nightmare in which every step is retarded by unseen obstacles and the universe is blacked out by a curtain of woe.

They passed the darkened shadows

of Martha's farm and much later made out the deep black shapes which were the buildings of Barker's Fork. It was with some sense of relief that they found themselves moving along the main street. There, the sheriff ordered a halt.

"Here, Joe, open up Moffat's grain store. It's empty this time of year. Door's only on the latch. It's the only place we got to put them until morning."

Lights moved towards the empty store. The wooden doors were swung open. Inside, men laid out boards along the floor and one by one the corpses were carried in and placed with as much reverence as possible in a row.

"That's it. Straighten that feller out a little and put the lady a bit away from the others — that's only decent. Hey, Billy, higher off the ground with Mr Russe. You're letting his arm drag through the dirt. Yeah, that's more like it."

Len, standing by his borrowed horse

in the moonlit street, looked around, startled, as he heard the name. At length, Holt and his men came back out. The doors were swung to and secured.

"OK. That'll have to do jest now. You two take the team around to the livery stables and see them settled. Git that feller Saunders out of his bed to open up. Bret, Beebo, remember and see me in the morning."

"Yeah. All right, Sam, I'll be there, but it's been one hell of a day!"

"And night!" grumbled Kelly.

"You said it!" agreed Holt.

The group dispersed, mostly breathing sighs of relief to have their grisly and tiring labour done for the time being. The sheriff eyed Len as if wondering what to do with him. Len saw him more clearly now than he had been able to do in the darkness and shifting movement of recent events. Holt was a tall man of lean build with a big nose and long jaw. He had demonstrated in his every word and gesture that he had authority over the rough men he commanded and that he expected to be obeyed and, seemingly, always was. Len could see that he would be a dangerous man to cross. He was not quite so certain, though, as to Holt's integrity. Was he just a strong and honest representative of the law or did he represent something not so straight? It could be, on the other hand, that these suspicions were based upon the resentment that Len still felt at the sheriff's attitude towards him. If so, if that was all it was, Len told himself, then the suspicion was unfounded. It was a lawman's job not to take too much on trust and, maybe, especially not wandering strangers like himself.

"What's on your mind, Finch?" The question was blunt and unfriendly.

"The man in the black coat — that Mr Russe?"

"Sure it is. You know him?"

"Nope, but I've heard."

"OK. We'll talk about it in the morning. Come on."

He led the way up the street to his office. A black man, lying asleep on the porch, jumped up at their approach and took charge of the horses, leading them around to the back of the building.

Holt mounted the few steps and unlocked the door. He put his lamp on the table and lit two others from it. The place was almost bare apart from essential articles of furniture, the only luxury being an old sofa against one wall. He pulled out a cheroot and puffed slowly and with relish. Then he turned to Len.

"You'll need to stay here tonight. That cell through there is comfortable enough. Bunk's all right. No, I ain't puttin' you under arrest. Jest bein' hospitable! I'll sleep through here."

Len was fumbling in his inside pocket, thinking that, since Mr Russe was dead, he had better give the sheriff the letter right now, so as to keep himself in the clear. His groping fingers found nothing, however, and he began a troubled search through his other pockets.

The sheriff stopped puffing on the cheroot and stared at him.

"You lost somethin', son?"

"Well, eh, thing is, I . . . well, some money I had. Jest a few cents. Must have dropped them some place."

Holt gave a short barking laugh.

"Don't worry about it. This here's free board and lodgings!"

Within a moment, Len found himself steered into the cell and the door slammed behind him. He was so taken up with his loss that he hardly heard the key being turned.

He sat down on the bunk, his head spinning with confusion and fatigue. Then he lay back. The sheriff had been right about the bunk, anyhow. It wasn't too bad. Sleep overcame him, brushing his worries from his mind.

3

HE awoke to the sound of voices and opened his eyes to see sunlight streaming into the cell and casting a shadow of the barred window upon the whitewashed wall. The sight of the bars shocked him into full alertness and he swung his legs to the floor, irritation flooding through him. He found the door still locked and rattled it impatiently.

The voices in the other room stopped and, a moment later, Holt came through, swinging keys in his hand. His long face was grimacing in amusement.

"Damn me, near forgot all about this here dangerous gunslinger!" He raised his voice in mock concern for the benefit of the men he had just left. "Think I should let this wild feller out?"

64

He turned the key to the accompaniment of guffaws from next door. Len, who was sensitive to ridicule, pushed past him and found himself facing Bret Williams and Beebo Kelly in the sheriff's office. In daylight, he saw that Williams was middle-aged, with grey hair which contrasted with his ruddy complexion. He looked a decent enough kind of man in spite of the temper he had displayed on the previous evening. Beebo Kelly, however, had a sinister look about him. He wore black clothing and carried a Colt very low on his hip. His hair was dark and untidy and there were several days of black stubble on his face. His eyes seemed to peer out from behind half-closed lids as if hoping to see without being seen.

They were both grinning broadly at Len's gun and belt which lay on the table and which had obviously been the object of amused discussion.

Len snatched up the gunbelt and immediately fastened it on, his cheeks reddening and resentment showing in his face.

"Didn't give ya permission to take thet gun back, son," drawled Holt, "but I guess it don't matter. It ain't so dangerous!"

"Could jest about hit a barn door if ya threw it!" yelped Kelly with contempt.

Len said nothing because there was nothing to say. He understood their amusement and their contempt. His anger was as much against himself for carrying such a gun as it was against them for ridiculing it.

"Don't get all het up, son." Holt spoke for the first time in a kindly way as if he sympathised and as if his suspicions of the night before had gone. "Here, help yourself to coffee." He pushed a tin mug across the table and indicated the pot on the stove. "So, Bret, you got the undertaker started?"

"Yeah, he's down there now, gettin' them fixed up decent. Only thing is, we don't know about the woman. Nobody ever seen her before. Must have been travelling on to Creetown or maybe Gore-Flats."

"Better send somebody up along to see if we can trace any kinfolk. Send Tracy. He's pretty sharp." Holt's demeanour returned to its natural gravity. "I'm goin' to Maria Theresa. Sooner we get there with the bad news the better. You come with me as well, Beebo, and I'm takin' the kid."

Len looked up from his coffee in surprise.

"Think you'd better come along, Finch. First-hand account is generally a good idea. Hey, give Jim a shout, will ya, Beebo? Tell him to bring my horse and the roan."

The trail to the Maria Theresa took much of the early part of the morning. Most of the time they rode in silence, each seemingly busy with his thoughts. Kelly looked as if sunk into a state of apathy. Holt appeared unhappy at being cast in the role of harbinger of terrible news. Len was greatly troubled at the prospect of being asked to give his account of the scene of the massacre to a grieving widow and, perhaps, family. What could he actually say that would relieve their suffering in the slightest degree? Should he tell everything or try to gloss it over in some way? Somehow, he believed that he would be asked for every gory detail, or else, why have him there at all? Holt could just as easily explain the circumstances of Russe's death as far as was known. He felt like bursting out and saying exactly that, but he did not want to give the impression that he might be attempting to shirk a duty which the dead man's family had imposed upon him in their time of sorrow.

As they rode through the morning, they passed lush meadows, kept moist by the irrigation from streams and ditches, upon which herds of fine cattle were grazing. Len lifted himself from his gloomy thoughts far enough to gaze with interest at these well-fed beasts which looked to him like the best he had ever seen.

"Fine stock, eh, Finch?" Holt had noted his interest and had roused himself from his own thoughts. "You know somethin' about cattle? Maria Theresa has the finest herds in the entire state, as far as I know. Hell of a big spread too. Stretches all the way to them hills and beyond."

"Bigger than ever since Mr Russe took over Bar T an' Crossford coupla' years back," added Kelly.

"Ya should see it in cattle drivin' time, though, Finch," went on Holt, with an enthusiasm that somehow seemed foreign to him. "Fine herds come in from the west all the time and rest and feed up before they push 'em on to the railhead at Jefferson Falls. Makes plenty outa' them as well as from their own stock. Richest family I ever heard of." He spoke without envy but with a kind of grudging respect. "And things will get even better when the railroad pushes through to Barker's Fork."

"Thet so?" Len was really interested. "When's it comin' through?"

"Don't rightly know. Been jawin' over it for a long time. It was in all the newspapers from the East but then kinda' died down. But it's comin'. No doubt about it!"

They relapsed into silence. Then Len ventured a thought.

"Won't be the same now though, I guess, with Mr Russe gone."

"Maybe not." Holt looked thoughtful.

"Damn-blasted Injuns!" Kelly rasped out in angry indignation. "Goddamn polecats — killing a good man like thet! Hope to hell they git the army ta wipe them out!"

Len swung around to face him. He had formed a dislike of Kelly and did not mind contradicting him by expressing what he had come to believe was the truth.

"Don't reckon it was Injuns."

Holt drew on the reins and looked

sharply at him. He spoke before Kelly could disagree.

"What makes you think thet, Finch?"

"Well, whoever heard of Injuns with no scalpin' or tomahawks and no stealin'?"

"How do you know what they might have stole?" protested Kelly.

"Don't know thet. But there was plenty left — especially the horses. Why didn't they take them?"

They rode on again in silence, Holt seeming to chew over Len's remarks while Kelly scowled at the ground. Len, for his part, almost regretted his outburst as it seemed to him that he had come too close to the matter of the missing letter, which brought him a sense of guilt every time he thought about it. Maybe he should just tell Mrs Russe that he had found the letter and then had lost it. He would feel an utter fool but at least that would be the truth. On the other hand, since the letter had vanished now, was there any point in mentioning it? What good would it do? Still, the widow had a right to know, there was no doubt about that, and he ought to be straight about it.

He was still wrestling with these thoughts when he caught his first glimpse of the Maria Theresa. It was still some distance away, but, even so, he knew that it was the grandest place he had ever seen. The house was large and mostly stone-built, surrounded by a shady veranda and studded with many fine windows. The main entrance was covered by a splendid portico supported by wooden columns, that reminded Len of a picture he had once seen in a school history book.

The house was surrounded by neat gravel paths, some of which led to stables and other outbuildings. The main driveway was broad, and flanked by carefully planted pines. To one side there stood a large sign with the name of the ranch carved out in huge letters.

Holt led the way up the drive, looking

neither to left or right, while Len and Kelly followed a little way behind. Anyone observing their approach could have guessed that they were on serious business.

When they were almost at the front door, an elderly man came forward and offered to take the horses. Holt dismounted first, just as a gentleman appeared on the front step. At least, he certainly looked like a gentleman to Len. He was richly dressed in white shirt and maroon waistcoat, a gold watch-fob and with a neatly trimmed black beard. In some way, he reminded Len of the dead feller who he had seen lying at the open door of the stagecoach.

"That's Mr Russe now," said Holt, in a half whisper. "You two wait here 'til you're called."

He went up the steps, while Len stared after him in astonishment. He watched as the two men engaged in a grave conversation. At one point the tall man turned and gripped one of the pillars tightly as if in shock. The talk continued and then the big feller suddenly called out "Injuns!" as if he could hardly believe it and turned to stare at Kelly and Len as if seeing them for the first time. He then motioned for them to come forward and they all went through the fine hallway and into a long room where Len stopped still in the doorway, suddenly overcome with amazement.

It was the most beautiful place he had ever been in or could ever have imagined. There was a magnificent table of polished oak and a row of chairs with elegantly carved backs. On the table stood a statuette, made of silver, of a man on horseback waving a sword. Around the walls were sofas and other chairs covered in embroidered cloth. There was a deep carpet on the floor, and a chandelier hanging from the centre of the ceiling caught the light and glittered in a thousand points as it tinkled in the slight draught from the open door. Above the marble fireplace was a painting of a regal-looking woman in a fine gown and with a coronet around her head. Other paintings showed scenes of soldiers in red and blue uniforms, fighting brave battles and dying without fear.

A nudge from Holt brought Len out of his trance and he accepted Russe's invitation to sit upon one of the wooden chairs beside Kelly, who seemed almost as ill at ease as he was.

For a few minutes Russe seemed overcome with grief, holding a silk handkerchief over his eyes and sobbing through his beard. Meanwhile his three visitors sat in awkward embarrassment.

Russe then got up abruptly from his chair and moved to the window where he looked out and spoke without turning round to face them.

"So, you reckon maybe it wasn't Injuns at all, Sam?"

"Don't think so, Mr Russe. Thing is, them arrows are all old. I've had a good look at them. The sinews around the heads are all dried out — and the moccasin too. And, as the young feller says, Injuns woulda' taken the horses, sure thing."

"What do you think, Beebo?"

"I think it was Injuns," replied Kelly stubbornly.

"Looks more like somebody pretendin' to be Injuns," insisted Holt. "Though what the hell for I don't know. Outlaws would generally jest shoot the stage up, steal whatever they wanted and then clear outa the territory."

"The sheriff's right, Beebo." Russe's voice was gruff. "Injuns don't make no sense."

There was a long silence. Then Russe raised his handkerchief again to his eyes.

"My brother. My poor dear brother, gunned down jest like that!" He swung around, his face suddenly contorted with rage. "We got to get them varmints, Sam! I want to see them swinging!"

"I'll do everything I can, Mr Russe, so help me."

They sat and discussed the matter for some time longer, then Russe suggested that Holt and Kelly should go around to the kitchen to get coffee and something to eat. Len would have liked to have gone as well but Russe motioned for him to stay.

"Jest like a word with the young feller, Sam."

When the two others had gone, Russe questioned Len further about what he had seen, asking to be given every detail no matter how unpleasant. Len could not tell him any more than Holt already had, and as for the letter Len had by this time decided not to mention it because there was something about Russe that made him feel that it would be a big mistake to do so. To his relief, the rancher did not seem to have been expecting any letter and made no mention of it.

"Sheriff tells me you've been stayin' at Mrs Benn's place? Fine woman, isn't she?" He smiled meaningly, a glint coming into his eyes. "Real pretty granddaughter, too. Jest about your age."

Len explained that he had not actually been staying at Benn's farm and took the opportunity of mentioning that he was on the lookout for work as a cowhand. Russe looked at him thoughtfully.

"You look like a smart young feller and I can nearly always use a good man. Not right now, though. It'll have to be later, when things get really busy; then there would be good prospects for a young man with ambition. You could become a top hand, once you show what you can do. Especially . . . " his voice dropped a little, almost as if he had decided to betray a confidence " . . when the railway comes through. The sky's the limit for a really smart man then. You heard about the railway?"

"Yeah, sheriff told me about thet."

"It's on its way. Now, you know the Benn place. Pretty rundown, ain't it? Mrs Benn's been struggling on with thet worn-out land for years and years. Poor old lady goin' to drop in her tracks one day if she don't let up. I've offered to buy the place, good price too, but she won't have it. Not that I made the offer jest out of charity, mind you. It's as much to my benefit as it is to hers. The railway's got to come right through thet part of the valley and I probably won't lose on the deal, but I offered her at least as much as the railway company would and that offer still holds. It would be a good thing for everybody concerned if she accepted, and she could use the money now and get some enjoyment out of life instead of waiting, maybe for years, if she lives to see it at all. It's no life there for a young girl, either, is it?"

"Maybe not," conceded Len.

"Well, suppose you go back there for a while and help out as best you can until I find you a real good job here. As a friend, with no axe to grind, you're more likely to be listened to than I am, because thet old lady, good woman though she is, has got more suspicion in her than a coyote sniffin' around a trap. You'd be doin' her a good turn if you got her around to taking the money and using it to give her and her granddaughter a decent life. And, who knows, Emma and you'll probably get on jest fine! Who knows what the future might bring!"

"Well." Len was not at all sure of his ground. What Russe said seemed to make some sense but he reckoned that his own influence on Martha was about zero and likely to remain so. On the other hand, he did not feel that he could argue with Russe about any of these matters if he was going to have any chance of achieving his ambitions — even the very limited ones of working with cattle and buying himself a new shirt, far less the grandiose visions which had just been presented to him. As for making it with Emma, well that seemed like pie in the sky! "I don't know, Mr Russe. Thing is, they hardly know me."

"They soon will." Russe's spirits seemed a little uplifted. "You'll fit in down there jest like one of the family, you mark my words. You jest get back there, soon as you can." He appeared to consider the matter settled and looked slowly around the room as if his attention had suddenly been caught up by the splendour of his surroundings. "What do you think of this place, young feller?"

"It's really somethin'," answered Len, with genuine admiration.

Russe seemed pleased by Len's awe-struck tone. He walked around the room, inspecting the various fine articles of furniture and ornaments as if seeing them for the first time, himself.

"All this," he waved his hand as if to take in the whole room. "All this is the best that money can buy. All of it came from Europe, from the finest houses, even from some of the palaces of Europe! You know somethin', Finch, our family goes back a long way. My ancestors came over from Europe more than a hundred years ago. My great-grandfather was an officer in the Imperial Guard of Her Majesty the Empress Maria Theresa of Austria-Hungary." He stopped and glanced sharply at Len, as if wondering if he was being understood. "She was the ruler of the greatest empire ever to rise to power in Europe. The Holy Roman Empire, it was called. Still goin' strong yet and it's lasted for a thousand years!"

Len said nothing. He felt pretty sure that Miss Trudy had never mentioned any Austrian empire. If she had, it had gone in one ear and out the other as far as he was concerned. Austria, as far as he could remember, had been mentioned in geography. It was one of them countries in Europe, right enough, but that was all he was certain about.

"You know much about history, young feller?"

"Some," Len answered defensively.

82

History with Miss Trudy had been the Revolution, George Washington and something about the Pilgrim Fathers. That was about it. He hadn't thought there was much more.

"That's what I thought." Russe nodded his head, seeming to understand. "Maria Theresa was empress when my ancestor was in the Imperial Guard. He reckoned he even had some blue blood himself, so that means that I . . . " He broke off and gazed with reverence at the queenly portrait above the fireplace. "Well, we always felt we were special as a family. We proved it too. After we came to this country, we worked our way up from nothing. My father had a place only about a tenth of the size of this, but when he died and Hans and I took over we built it up and bought out other ranches until we have all this!" He stalked to the window and gazed across his corrals and fences to the open range beyond. "All this!"

He stood upright, his shoulders set back, head tilted, looking not unlike an emperor himself as he gazed over his dominions. To Len, it seemed as if he reckoned that he owned just about the entire United States and it wouldn't be long before he got the rest of it. For a moment, too, it was as if Russe forgot that he was not alone as he lifted down a richly decorated scabbard from the wall and drew out the long, shining blade of a sabre. He waved this weapon about in the air, making movements which suggested that he would like nothing better than the chance to cut off some poor feller's head with it, and then replaced it hastily as he saw Len's eyes upon him.

"That was my great-grandfather's sword," he explained unnecessarily. His manner became stern and determined, like a man greatly wronged who means to fight back. "Tell you somethin', Finch, I won't ever give up. I'll build up the Maria Theresa greater than ever before, for my brother's sake as well as for the family name. And while I'm doin' it. I'll see them murderin' skunks dead, every one of them! You take it from me! But here . . . " he adopted a kindly tone of concern . . . "I been borin' you out of your mind with all my talk. You get around now to the kitchen for some refreshment. You look all tuckered out. Sheriff says you were all up half the night gettin' in the stage. Thanks for everything you've done, son. I won't forget it and, here, take this." He thrust a ten-dollar bill into Len's hand. "No, no, I insist! Buy some clothes or whatever you think you need. Remember to be real nice to the ladies. They could do with some good advice from a smart man.

Len found his way to the kitchen just as the two others were coming out. As they were mounting up, Russe appeared again in front of the house and asked Kelly to stay behind for a little while to look at a horse that seemed feverish.

As Len rode off down the drive with Holt, he asked if Beebo Kelly knew such a lot about horses that his advice was in such demand.

"Could be," grunted Holt, non-committally.

When they reached Barker's Fork, the sheriff took the roan, along with his own horse, and told the negro to stable them both.

"Sorry I can't let ya have him any longer, Finch, but he needs restin'. Suppose you'll be goin' back to Martha's for your pony. Shouldn't take you too long."

Len trudged through the little town, feeling less than enthusiastic at the prospect of a long walk. As he went, he was aware of the stares of some of the better-dressed townspeople, who looked at his shabby clothes as if he was a tramp. When he passed a lady on the sidewalk she steered her skirts well out of the way as if he might contaminate her fine outfit. After that, he walked in the street with the horses. He stopped only once, to stare into the window of Morgan's Gun Store which had a display of rifles and hand-guns.

They all seemed pretty expensive and he thrust the ten-dollar bill deeper into his pocket and kept going.

By the time he reached the farm he was tired, footsore and hungry. He met Emma at the gate. She had just climbed over the fence from the vegetable patch and now stood, leaning on her rake with one arm and her other on her hip. Somehow, she managed to look provocative and hostile at the same time. He flinched slightly in anticipation of her sarcasm.

"Well, blow me if it ain't thet hot-shot cowboy! I thought you were runnin' things at the Maria Theresa by now!"

"Well, thing is, they ain't needin' any more hands!"

"Even a real smart feller like you! If thet don't beat all!"

"OK. I never said nothin' about bein' hot-shot."

"You're too modest, Mr Finch, far too modest! Anyhow, why are you back here? Forgit somethin'?"

"I left my pony."

"Sure you did. Well, jest take it and get goin'."

"Listen, Emma, I need work. Do you think Martha might take me on?"

"This place is half mine, do you know thet? Martha and me both do the hirin' and firin'."

He noticed, in spite of her words and her manner, that a smile played around the corners of her mouth. Without much more banter she led him in to see her grandmother and, before long, the matter was settled. He would work for his keep and whatever they could afford to pay him. Also, he would sleep in the barn. There was plenty to do. Red hadn't shown up to do any of the odd jobs and Lee Sanger was getting slower every day.

Len accepted the position gratefully and worked long and hard. As the days stretched into a couple of weeks he got to know Emma better and learned to return her impudent remarks with humour of his own. Never once did

88

he raise the matter that Russe had put into his head. The idea of trying to suggest to either Martha or Emma what they should do about selling their farm now made even less sense to him than it had up at the Maria Theresa. They were too independent and too certain in their own minds that they were doing the right thing in keeping the place going, no matter how poor it was — and it was poor, there was no doubt about that. Len had seen farms like it before, run-down places, with little money coming in and no chance of improvement. He had seen them vanish and become rough grazing, and, felt sure it would happen here too.

But still he did not say anything because he guessed that there was some other reason behind the refusal to take Russe's offer. One morning when he and Emma were walking out to the upper pasture, he discovered what it was.

"Place gets harder all the time," she remarked in a rare moment of depression. "But we ain't movin'. You heard about the railroad and the offer we got from Maria Theresa?"

Len admitted that he had, and then Emma told him about all the trouble. Kurt Russe had made them an offer before anybody had heard about the railroad coming. It had been a poor offer and they had refused even though they were puzzled at his interest in the place. After that, things had got worse. Fences had been cut, fires started, horsemen had ridden through their crops in the night. Then it had come out in the newspapers about the railroad and Russe had made a better offer because everybody knew that land values would have to rise. They had refused that too because they knew that the Kellys had been doing the damage and that the Maria Theresa was behind it. The Kellys were a family of four brothers, poor, mean and wild. Emma had recognized them in the night, as you can often recognize a man by his build and way of sitting in the saddle, even in the half light and masked though he is. The Kellys were out to hire to whoever would pay them. Only Kurt Russe was interested in the farm and it was easy to guess that he knew about the plans of the railway company before most folks did. So Martha had said she would die before giving in to him and his hirelings.

That afternoon Len rode his old pony slowly all the way to the Maria Theresa. When he got there he gave Russe back his ten-dollar bill and then turned back for the farm, feeling the rancher's eyes burning into his back and knowing he had made an enemy.

4

OLD SKIN awakened in the half light of dawn with his mind still full of the tales of the dream spirits who had taken him back to the old time. Their stories had been dark and troublesome. He had seen himself again as a young man, coming to the white hunters and tasting their whiskey and helping them to kill the buffalo. The white people, he was told, needed many buffalo to feed the men who put down the iron trail for the monster, as he had then thought of it. The iron track had stretched far across the plains and there had been many mouths to feed and the slaughter of the buffalo had been beyond his wildest imaginings. Their bones had scattered like snow so that it seemed that there would soon come a time when there were no more and then the Indians of the plains must starve.

Those Indians who had hunted with himself for the white men and their trade goods tired of it and returned to their villages, and then Redwing had found himself as a lone Indian in the camps of the whites because one morning he awoke to discover that Little Bead Woman had gone too and had said no word because she knew that the hot spirit held sway in her husband's mind and he could not leave it. Then Redwing had sunk low and was no longer a hunter but was put to skinning the buffalo as if he were an old squaw. The months and years had gone by in this labour, relieved only by the nightly oblivion brought by the whiskey, and he knew himself to be as a dog to the white men.

The dream spirits, too, in their wickedness, brought back to him the day when a band of Pawnee had ridden slowly past the skinning-camp and he had looked up to see the contempt in their eyes and knew himself to be an outcast for ever, like a ghost who finds the tepee door stitched up against him.

So he awoke and sat up with his head full of sorrow and crawled out into the morning, glad to leave the dream spirits to their darkness. Today was a new day and he must live it as it came to him. Whiskey, that enemy and friend, was never far from his mind and he thought of the silver dollar that still lay hidden in the envelope that had come into his hand when the young feller had fallen on top of him.

His old fingers trembled with excitement at the thought of how much spirit a silver dollar could buy as he ripped open the envelope, with its crazy sign-talk, and pulled out the dollar into the dim light of the early day.

It was like no dollar he had ever seen. The eagle traced upon it looked as if carved from wood, with stiff wing feathers and a stiff fan tail, but the strangest thing about it was its two

94

heads, facing east and west, as if in two minds which way to fly, and with tongues shooting out from open beaks like those of snakes tasting the air.

Skin looked at this design in wonder for a few moments and then turned the piece over and found himself staring at Little Bead Woman.

He closed his eyes then, thinking that the dream spirits had returned, perhaps better-disposed towards him, and then opened them once more to find her still there, with her mouth seeming to smile a little at his foolishness.

It was as if she sat in a pool of light, silvery and shining, like a face in the moon. Her head looked to one side and yet one eye was turned slightly towards him with that amused expression which he knew of old. He could see that she had reached a maturity in his absence. There was more fat under her chin and there were little lines under her eyes, but there was no mistaking her nose and her ears, her hair and the calmness of her features . . . It was

Little Bead Woman grown older and with the dignity that comes with age and that was as it should be, and it gave him great satisfaction to see her as she was now and not just as the girl who had deserted him in his youth.

He gazed at the portrait for a very long time, admiring every line and detail, and observed with awe that Little Bead Woman seemed as if she had been carved from snow and was standing on a lake of ice. All of the picture glittered and gleamed and sparkled like the light from heaven and he knew that the dream spirits had brought it to him to let him know that all was not yet lost.

He sat and wondered about this for much of the morning and he began to feel sure that a power dream was on its way to tell him of his future. With that in mind, he put the silver picture safely into his pocket and went off downstream to the high point overlooking the range, and stayed there for three days and nights without food and with little water and waited for his dreams to speak. By the middle of the fourth day, however, he realized that the dream spirits had no more to say and he concluded that they could see no sense in speculating on the future of an old Indian who did not have any. That, though, brought him a feeling of comfort because it meant that his journey would soon be at its end.

So he went back up the valley and to the Johnstone place and was given a little food and worked hard at the wood-chopping until he had enough money to go into the town and buy his whiskey. But the strange silver dollar remained in his pocket.

After that, he made his way to Martha's place.

They saw him just as they came out of the house after their midday meal. Emma spotted him first.

"Hey, Red, where have ya been? Hey, Red!"

"He ain't hearin' you, child," observed Martha.

"Hey, Red! Red! Hey, Skin! . . . Hey, Redskin!"

"Don't give the old feller any of your sass," snapped Martha.

"I'll go and speak to him," said Len, much to their surprise, and he hurried off along the narrow path before they could say anything further.

They met halfway along by the maize field. Skin saw the young feller coming and noted that he looked a sight cleaner than he had done before. He was wearing a clean shirt and pants, both a little too large for him, and had shaved the youthful stubble from his face. The clothes had belonged to Emma's father and had come out of the large box that Martha kept in her bedroom, where they had been since both he and his wife had died in the river accident. Skin knew about the box because Martha had once given him a shirt out of it, which he still wore.

"Say, Red." Len kept his voice low in the hope that it would not float back to the house "Do you have anythin' belongin' to Kurt Russe?"

Skin looked at him closely. He knew perfectly well what was being referred to. In a way, he had expected this from the young feller but his mind had already switched back to the two weeks of hard labour he had done up at the Maria Theresa about a couple of years ago and he remembered with clarity that when he had asked for his pay the foreman had told him that the big boss had not thought to leave it for him. And he remembered, too, that the big boss had been too busy to be disturbed over such a small matter and that a little further argument had resulted in old Skin being shouted at and pushed and driven out like a dog being chased away from the fire.

It seemed to him, also, that even yet he had not been paid. The silver picture of Little Bead Woman could not possibly have come from Kurt Russe. Little Bead Woman and Kurt Russe lived in two different worlds and could have no possible connection with one another. The little siver moon had been drawn from the night sky by the dream spirits in order to tell him something about himself and Little Bead Woman. Kurt Russe had no place in any of it. It would be like inviting a wild hog to the wedding-feast. He felt like saying something like this to the young feller but believed that it would be a waste of time. The young feller, after all, was white and, therefore, wouldn't be able to see things quite straight and as they really were.

"No." His voice carried the conviction of his heart. "I don't have anythin' that belongs to Kurt Russe."

When they got back to the house, they found that Lee Sanger had gone home early and had said that he would not be back because he was going to work up at the Maria Theresa for better money.

Martha said she reckoned that this was when the trouble was about to start again. Things had been quiet over the last few weeks ever since news of the stage had come in and there had been a lot of things going on, what with the big, fancy funeral for Hans Russe, and Holt leading posses all over the country in the hope of catching the wild Indians or white outlaws or whatever they were. Sanger's departure, though, seemed to her to suggest a return to a vindictive turn of mind up at the Maria Theresa. There was no way that Sanger would have been offered employment there except as a means of depriving the Benn place of his help, poor enough though that was.

She was proved right a few nights later when the ripening maize crop was ridden through and trampled pretty bad by three or four horsemen. Martha set her face into an expression of calm determination. Emma was white with anger and she brought out the only firearm they had, a light squirrel-rifle, and set it up in the porch.

"Next time they come around here, I'll be ready for them," she vowed. "We have a right to defend our property.

"Don't know if Holt will see it that way," commented Martha.

"You ever told the sheriff about any of this?" asked Len.

"Sure." Emma's voice was ringing with contempt. "He sent Williams around and asked a few questions. That was all! No proof, he said, no proof! What the blazes . . . "

"Here, mind your language, girl!" interrupted her grandmother.

That afternoon, Len made an excuse and rode into town. He stopped outside Morgan's Gun Store, tied up his pony and went inside. Morgan, thin, moustached, somehow anxious-looking, came forward.

"What can I do fer you? Mr Finch, ain't it?"

Len brought out all the money he had, including what he had earned over the last few weeks. It amounted to six dollars and fifteen cents.

"I want to buy a gun but this is all I got."

Morgan shook his head.

"Cheapest handgun I have costs fifteen dollars. Sorry."

As Len returned to the street he saw that three riders had stopped outside the store close to the spot where he had hitched his pony. They were, undoubtedly, the most disreputable bunch of men he had ever seen. They were dirty, unkempt, with long straggling hair and two had untidy beards. The third was younger and wore a black moustache which hung over his broad lips. All were dark and brown-eyed. Each carried a heavy Colt on his hip.

Len knew at once who they were although he had never before set eyes on them.

One of the older men grinned broadly as Len appeared.

"Hey, fellers, here's thet gunslinger from the Benn place!"

"Keep your goddamn head down, Abe, for Christ-sake or he'll blow it off!" yelled one of his brothers. "He kin hit a barn door without even pullin' the trigger!"

Len said nothing but moved forward to unhitch the pony. The younger man urged his horse towards him.

"Don't tell me you're gonna ride this lump o'dog-meat! Thet's real unkind." He pulled out his gun and waved it mockingly. "Seems to me it'd be a mercy ta kill it off now 'stead o' makin' it walk any further."

Len mounted up and rode slowly along the street in the general direction of the farm. He was aware of the three riders following behind him. After a few minutes, his route led him through a narrow lane and it was there that they suddenly overtook him and ranged themselves across his path. They said nothing. The older one had sly eyes like Beebo Kelly, he noted; the younger man's eyes seemed more alert but cold and empty of feeling.

"Stand outa' the way," snapped Len, anger rising within him.

"You don't want to talk to us like

thet," objected the one called Abe. "Thet ain't nice, is it, fellers?" Len saw him drawing a heavy leather whip from his saddle. "You gotta learn to talk polite."

"Thing is, Abe, thet this feller's a gunslinger. He's used ta shovin' his way around," chuckled the younger man. "Folks move outa' his way or he fills them full o' lead."

"Maybe he could do with a whippin'."

"Whip's no good against a gunslinger. He don't understand nothin' but guns — guns and purty gals. Thet so' Finch — you been havin' a party with little Emma, down on the farm?"

"Shut your dirty mouth!" rapped Len, knowing that he was providing the opening they had been angling for but unable to make a more docile reply.

They moved forward as a body. A hand slapped hard across his face. A fist struck into his stomach. Fingers grabbed the back of his shirt and he was dragged from the saddle to fall into the dirt. When he struggled to his feet, he saw that they had all dismounted and that the youngest man was standing in the middle of the lane, arms akimbo and a contemptuous grin on his lips.

"OK, Finch, time to make your move.

Len realized what he was up against. The quarrel had been instigated and the challenge made. The witnesses were standing by. Two armed men faced one another in the quiet lane. The fact that he was armed only with a piece of useless metal would make no difference. A gun carried can only be seen as a gun ready for action, and who would be left to argue that he had not made the first move?

So the stage was set for murder, with every person present knowing what the outcome must be. Even so, he did not regret that the rusted old gun was at his hip. He had strapped on the gunbelt that day in the hope that he would ride back with an efficient weapon in the holster. The gun had been left in its place partly out of habit and partly because an empty holster just looks strange, like a cowboy on the summer range without his hat or wearing the wrong kind of boots. It was as simple as that and it would not have made any difference anyhow. Since the Kellys wanted to take him, they would have done it one way or another even without the pretence that he was armed, and in any case he would not have left the gun at home just in the hope that they might leave an unarmed man alone.

The three were standing still, breathing audibly through their mouths and staring at him, eyes half closed, leering lips curling at the edges. He knew that they were waiting for him to show fear. That they would enjoy. The realization made him all the more determined to give them no such satisfaction and he allowed no trace of the fear of death which was welling up inside him to flicker into his face.

Moments passed and then the brother called Abe shuffled his feet and spoke.

"Tell ya what, Pete, I'll count to three an' then ya let him have it."

"I'm with ya." The young man grinned in delight.

"Here we go then. One, two . . . " Len knew that he was going to go for the rusted old gun just as if it was new, well-oiled and ready. The gesture seemed important. It showed a willingness to fight rather than just to stand and take it. " . . . three!"

Len's fingers touched the butt of his gun at the same second as the Colt appeared in his opponent's hand. The barrel pointed straight at him. The finger whitened on the trigger. Len steeled himself for the terrible impact of the bullet and then dropped his gun to the ground as the heavy leather whip snaked out and struck him a hatchet-like blow across the face.

The world seemed suddenly on fire. All was red and burning. Pain stabbed through his mind like a spear-point and he fell to his knees as the red gave quick way to black and he struggled to retain consciousness. He held on in the darkness as the red-hot stone that was his eyeball burned into his skull. He was only dimly aware of confused sound around him, the trampling of hooves, harsh voices raised in laughter.

"Next time, Finch, we'll take your head off!"

"Best git back to where ya came from, Finch, afore we git real mad and tear your heart out!"

By slow degrees he forced open the eye which had not been struck and looked through a wall of tears into the hardened mud of the lane. Then he got to his feet and staggered to the side of the nearest building. He leaned up against it and tentatively explored his eye and face. Blood trickled down his fingers and wrist and into his sleeve from the cut in his cheek, and his right eye was a mass of swelling pain.

"Hey, you all right, mister?" A small thin man with a worried expression stood beside him. "Ya look pretty bad."

"Well . . . " Len found it hard to twist his mouth into speech. "I guess . . . Listen, is there a pony around here, someplace?"

"Yeah, down at the end of the lane. I'll get it for ya."

Len mounted the pony with difficulty and made a faltering progress through the outskirts of the town and on to the trail leading in the direction of the farm. The sight of his left eye gradually cleared but his right was as firmly closed as if a boot stood upon it. When he eventually reached the farm, Emma and her grandmother took him in hand, asking no questions and saying little until his wound had been bathed and his eye and face bandaged. Only then did they ask for an account of the incident. Len outlined what had happened while Martha sighed and shook her head.

"Thet Pete Kelly! Hard to believe thet he used to come around here when he was little. Used to be quite sweet on Emma too. He even said he would come a'courtin' when he was older!"

"Jest as soon have a wart-hog comin' around courtin' as him!" exploded Emma in sudden rage.

"Thet's just about what you told him at the time, as I remember," recollected Martha. "Now he's jest gone as bad as his brothers. Vicious as the rest of them."

"You said it," grunted Len through his pain.

The remainder of that day and all of the next went by without further trouble. Len worked as well as he could although the lack of sight in one eye seemed to make every task six times as hard. The pain also kept him awake most of the night, therefore he urged Emma to go to her bed instead of taking her turn keeping a lookout as they had planned. It was in the very early hours of the third morning after his encounter with the Kellys that he heard a shot from somewhere at the back of the house. He went to investigate quickly but with caution, the light squirrel-rifle at the ready.

For some minutes he scanned the surrounding yards and fields, acutely aware of the difficulty imposed by his poor sight, especially in the dim, grey light of dawn. He saw no movement but heard a sound that seemed to drift towards him from some little distance. It was a kind of moaning and wheezing and it seemed to be coming from the direction of the south paddock. Suddenly full of apprehension, he ran towards it and then slowed down and approached quietly and with a sinking heart.

The old cow-pony lay on its side, the last remnants of its life dribbling from the wound made by the rifle-bullet.

It died as he watched it and within a few moments. His hands gripped the fence while sorrow and anger flooded through him; sorrow because he was witnessing its final pain and death throes, anger at the callous killing of the innocent animal in an act of spite against himself.

"Dog-meat, is it, Kelly? I'll tear the hearts out of the dogs that did this; and yours, too, Russe!"

The two women, wakened by the shot, saw him leaning across the fence of the south paddock, his head in his hands.

That night the fencing on the far side of the east meadow was torn down and scattered. They heard the noise of it and Emma loosed off a shot in that direction and was answered by hoots and yells and the sound of pistols being fired in the air. They spent all of the next day repairing the damage but the next morning it was down again, worse than ever. This time it could not be repaired without buying in more materials so they left the mess scattered where it was and turned back to the house, each with the unspoken thought that the Kellys were beginning to come out on top.

"We got to bring in the sheriff!"

exclaimed Len. "He's supposed to keep law and order. Why not get him to do it?"

"We can bring him here to see the mess but then he's goin' to ask where to start lookin'," said Martha. "We know who's doin' it but then he's goin' to ask how we can see Kellys in the dark when it could be anybody."

"Still, it's up to him to do somethin' about it. This Sam Holt, what do you think of him? Straight and honest?"

Martha hesitated. "Hard to say. I used to think he was a good man but now I'm not so sure. Too many people around these parts dancin' to the tune of the Maria Theresa these days, and after he made Beebo Kelly a deputy I reckoned that somebody was startin' to lead him around by the nose. Thet Beebo Kelly's the brightest in the family but thet's not sayin' much! A Kelly's a Kelly and they don't make good lawmen."

Len thought about going to see the sheriff that day, but did not do so, partly because of the amount of work to be done around the farm but mostly because Martha's words had reinforced the feeling of distrust of Holt which had always been present in him.

That night, the trouble started earlier than usual. At about midnight they heard the sound of hoofbeats from the back of the house and looked out to see a light approaching at speed across the meadow. With a start, they realized that there was a horseman carrying a lighted torch out before him, holding it at a low angle to keep it alight, and obviously making for the straw-filled barn.

Len leapt out of the window and ran to intercept him but did not reach the vicinity of the barn quickly enough to prevent the man from hurling the torch towards it. Luckily, it was a poorly judged throw, possibly because the raider was put off at the sudden appearance of Len or because a flame from the torch had touched his hand, and the lighted brand tumbled through the air without reaching the door of the barn. Instead it fell into some straw lying on the ground outside and instantly set fire to it.

The rider turned his horse aside just as Len prepared to make a grab at him and began to retreat rapidly the way he had come. He had not gone far when a shot rang out from the back door of the house where Emma had appeared with the light rifle. Len saw the man jerk in the saddle, sway wildly, clutch at the pommel and then begin to fall across his horse's neck. Confused and frightened, the animal came to a slithering halt and the rider was thrown to the ground.

Len ran as fast as he could over the rough grass, half blinded as he was in the poor light and by his dependence on only one eye, and reached the man just as he struggled to his feet and was attempting to remount. Len's groping hands found some part of his clothing and he held on as the man struggled to release himself. There was the sound of ripping cloth and Len felt his enemy breaking away from him. The man had now succeeded in putting one foot into the stirrup and was pulling himself back into the saddle, regardless of the amount of torn waistcoat that he left in Len's hands. For a moment, it seemed that the cloth would hold long enough for Len to bring the man down, but then it ripped further and at the same time a fist, swung wildly backwards, struck into the bandage over Len's wounded eye and the savage pain caused him to let go.

The raider was now fully mounted and urged his horse away, but at that moment a second bullet flew by very close to his ear. He turned his head to see Emma now just a short distance away and with her rifle still aimed at him. For a few seconds his face, stripped now of its mask, showed against the light of the stars.

She recognized him at once as Pete Kelly and shrank back a little and lowered her empty rifle as he drew his sidegun and aimed it towards her. He seemed to hesitate, raising and aiming the barrel two or three times in rapid succession as if unable to make up his mind; then he turned it on Len and loosed off two shots, one of which tore across his shoulder, opening up the skin and sending a torrent of blood into his shirt.

Then, with a groan of pain, Kelly pulled savagely at the reins and forced his mount around. Within a few seconds he had vanished into the darkness.

"You hurt bad, Len?" Emma's voice was full of anxiety.

"Jest a graze, feels like," grunted Len in reply.

When they got back to the house, they found that Martha had managed to put out the fire with buckets of water and a broom before it could reach serious proportions. On examination, Len's wound turned out to be as he had said, just a graze, but a painful and bloody one for all that.

They sat in the light of the kitchen lamp, feeling drained at the sudden emergency and the danger that had passed so close to them. Emma looked white and strained but she reloaded the gun with quiet determination.

"Thet was Pete Kelly," she said, as she thrust the cartridges home. "Did you recognize him!"

"Couldn't see a thing after he hit me in the eye," answered Len ruefully.

"I wounded him."

"He's carrying your bullet," agreed Len.

5

IN the morning Len had the feeling that a new and even more dangerous phase had been reached in their battle against the Kellys. It seemed obvious to him that their anger and vindictiveness must reach a higher point now that one of their number had been wounded, and they would no longer be attacking just because Russe was paying them to do so but now they must be goaded on to more savage deeds by a desire for revenge.

He found himself to be increasingly anxious as to the safety of Emma who had pulled the trigger against Pete Kelly and would be likely to have become the particular object of their hatred. He felt like telling her to remain out of sight in the house as much as possible but he knew that he would be wasting his breath. Emma was too proud of spirit to skulk indoors for fear of men whom she despised.

They went all around the farm at first light, looking out for further signs of damage but finding none. It was as if the night's setback had acted as a discouragement for the Kellys, but no-one on the farm had any doubt that they would soon be back and that this time the defenders would have to fight, not just for their property but in all probability for their lives.

After breakfast, Len stepped out of doors again, ready to begin work. He had slept little after the midnight attack, and the pain of his grazed arm had joined forces with the renewed aching in his eye so that he felt generally unfit and not far from exhaustion. Not that he would have made that any excuse for working less hard that day than he usually did. The fight that Emma and Martha were putting up was one that he accepted fully as his own and he would not have thought of shirking from any part of it.

He took a few breaths of the morning air and caught the smell of the burnt straw which was blowing about the yard in the slight breeze. The scent brought back the events of the night with greater force to his mind and, with something of that impulse which causes old warriors to revisit ancient battlefields, he began to retrace his steps across the meadow to the spot where he had struggled with Pete Kelly. When he got there, he saw that the grass had been well beaten down in the fight and the earth churned by the hooves of the frightened horse.

Something black came into the line of vision of his left eye and he bent down to pick up a piece of cloth which appeared to be a strip torn from a waistcoat. To his surprise, his hand came into contact with something hard which lay concealed in the grass. His fingers groped further and he gripped a short length of chain. He straightened up then and discovered that he held in his hand a fine gold watch.

His face registered stupefied amazement as he turned it over in his hands. The dew-covered gold case and chain glittered richly in the morning sun. It was beautiful and expensive and not in any way the kind of object which somebody like Pete Kelly would be likely to possess. It was, however, exactly the kind of object that a Kelly might have in his possession once given an opportunity of stealing it.

He wiped the tears from his one open eye, which was still much inclined to water, and examined the face of the watch with its fine roman numerals and delicate gold decoration. He then turned it around and read the name engraved on the back of the case.

It stated with absolute clarity: Hans Wilhelm Russe.

When he placed the watch on the kitchen table, the two women looked at it in silence for a few moments before Martha spoke.

"Thet's a terrible thing to see," she said.

A little later in the forenoon, Len borrowed one of their horses and rode into Barker's Fork. As he made his way along the main street he found himself keeping his one eye well open and on the alert for the Kellys, so he was not unduly surprised to see one of them leaning up against a veranda post just outside the saloon. It was one of the three brothers he had faced up to in the deserted lane, the one who had stood by as Pete threatened him with the gun and Abe had struck him with the whip. Len thought Martha had said that this brother's name was Saul Kelly. He seemed like the oldest, with lined features and streaks of grey coming into his dirty hair. His beard was long and matted, and tobacco-stained from the pipe held between his ugly teeth. As Len approached, he leaned out over the street and spat slowly and deliberately.

"Be closin' both yer eyes pretty soon, Finch, permanent!"

Len felt his heart turning black with

anger. He slowed his horse and then stopped within feet of the man. He too leaned over the street and spat in the same manner and onto the same spot as had Saul Kelly.

"You got it comin', Kelly," he said, the darkness of his anger shading his voice.

When he reached the sheriff's office he went in without knocking. Holt was sitting at his desk writing something into a log-book and glanced up in some surprise. His face began to split into a sardonic grin.

"What in hell happened to you, Finch, been buttin' heads with a longhorn?"

Len was in no mood for humour. He sat down on the seat opposite without invitation and set his eye steadily on Holt's smirking face.

"Nothin' to do with longhorns; it's all got to do with Kellys."

He described in a few words his confrontation with the Kelly brothers in the lane and then, with growing vehemence, the attacks upon the farm, the damage, the attempt at arson, the struggle with Pete Kelly and finally the exchange of shots.

"Well, it all sounds pretty bad," commented Holt in an unconcerned tone that belied his words. "But what do ya have in the way of evidence thet the Kellys are behind it? You've only seen men galloping around in the dark. You say thet Emma recognized Pete Kelly, even in the middle of the night, but when it gets right down to it, it's only her word against his . . . "

"What in God's name do ya need ta get you off thet chair and out to help folks thet are in danger? Do ya have to see these two women stretched out dead and full o' bullets before you'll do anythin'? What kind of a goddamn sheriff are you?"

Holt turned white with anger. He began to rise from the table, fists clenched, but stopped as Len produced the gold watch and placed it before him.

"Read thet inscription," snapped Len.

Holt did so and then looked at Len in speechless astonishment, his eyes searching for an explanation.

"That watch," Len said slowly and clearly as if explaining something to a person of limited understanding, "came out of Pete Kelly's waistcoat when I was fightin' with him in Martha's meadow."

Holt examined the watch with care. For a long time he said nothing, then he looked at Len, eyes narrowed.

"You pulled this off Pete Kelly?"

"Yeah."

"Anybody see ya pull it off him?"

"For Christ sake!" Len felt his temper blazing up afresh. "What do ya need — a whole jury standin' around takin' notes?"

"Button up your lip, boy! Don't try to tell me my job! I've got plenty on my plate tryin' to get them four stage murders solved, as it is, and not gettin' anywhere fast. Now you come here, tellin' me thet the Benn place is being shot up and burned down by the Kellys. Why in hell would they want ta do thet? What good's it goin' ta do them? Then ya bring out this watch belongin' ta Hans Russe and tell me thet Pete Kelly had it. How would he get it?"

Len had not thought to see such nervous agitation in Holt. His relaxed, in-control demeanour seemed to have deserted him.

"Figure that out for yourself. While you're at it, take a good look at Pete Kelly. Ask him how he got thet bullet-hole." Len spoke now to the sheriff with an assurance that had not been possible in any of their previous encounters. "Go up to the Maria Theresa. See Kurt Russe."

He stopped as he saw the steely look return to Holt's eyes. The sheriff stood up, hand going almost instinctively to his gun.

"I don't need some whippersnapper of a kid to hand out orders to me."

Holt's voice was suddenly cold and threatening. "I'll look into the situation at Martha Benn's place and I'll check on this watch and I'll ask the Kellys some questions and I'll do all of it, without you shootin' your mouth off! Now you've said enough so git goin'. If I want to ask you any questions, I'll let ya know."

Len rode back out of the town with mixed feelings. He was glad that he had put things in front of the sheriff but less pleased that he had not managed to do it in a more amicable way. Quarrelling with Holt could be of no help. Also there was something about the sheriff that left Len feeling less than convinced that decisive action would be taken. He reminded Len of a horse coming up to jump a fence with a look in its eye which questioned the wisdom of attempting it. There was something in front of Holt that he balked at and Len had the idea flickering in his mind that it was always the name Kurt Russe.

When he returned to the farm, he

gave an account of the meeting with the sheriff. Martha and Emma listened and smiled a little as Len admitted losing his temper. The fact that Holt had not returned with Len to the farm and had not promised immediate action did not seem to surprise them.

"What he'll do," prophesied Martha, "is send out Beebo Kelly to talk to his brothers. In thet way, he'll get the kind of answer that'll make it unnecessary for him to do much about it. As for the watch, well, it's not so easy to be sure about thet. Thet's a weird thing. Kind of thing thet could hang somebody."

A week went by and nothing was heard from the sheriff but, to their relief, nothing was heard from the Kellys either. They were not, however, lulled into any false sense of security. The trouble would return with a vengeance. Of that they were all convinced. Nevertheless, they made the best of the respite, and worked harder than ever to put the place to rights and to carry on with the normal farm work.

One day, Len went back into the town, this time with the mule-cart as it had been decided that some fencing materials must be bought in to repair the damage which had been done by the Kellys. He got the wood and wire and posts from a store near the edge of the town and spent all the money that Martha had provided for the purpose. He felt tempted to go in to ask Holt whether or not any progress had been made in his investigations, but the instinct to keep his head well down rather than take the risk of it being shot at prevailed and he turned for home without venturing into the main street.

He had not gone far, however, when he realized that his visit had not gone unobserved. Just on the outskirts of the town he glanced back to check that his load was quite steady and noticed a horseman some distance behind. There was something vaguely familiar about the man but, since he obviously was not a Kelly, Len was not concerned.

It was some time later when he turned around again and saw that he was still being followed. The man made no attempt to catch up on the slow-moving cart until they were more than a mile from Barker's Fork and then he began gradually to shorten the distance. As he drew level, Len recognized him as Morgan, the man who owned the gun store.

"Hey, Mr Finch." The slightly nervous manner that Len had observed in the gun store had reached a higher pitch. "I thought it was you. Saw you loadin' up your cart. Listen, I want you to take this." To Len's amazement, he produced a hand-gun from under his coat and passed it over, his hand jerking a little as he did so. "I found it in the back shop, later on, after you had gone. It's second-hand, o'course, but good. It's a Colt 44. Belonged to a feller called Wilson from over at Gore Flats. I bought it from his widder a couple of years back. You kin have it for ten dollars." Len opened his mouth to speak but Morgan waved a hand as if to silence him. "No, I don't want your money jest now. Pay me later, any time, when you have it. Take this too." He rummaged in his capacious pockets and brought out a small box of ammunition which he tossed into Len's outstretched hands. "I forgot all about thet gun when you was in. You take it. It's pretty good."

As he spoke, he turned his horse around until it had completed a half circle and he was facing back the way he had come. He hesitated for just a second before moving off.

"I know what you're up against, Mr Finch. Deputy Williams told me somethin' about it. Give my kindest regards to the ladies."

He rode away at speed while Len yelled out his surprised thanks. After the man had gone, Len held the gun in his hand, feeling its weight, spinning the chamber. His delight showed in his face and he grinned as he swung the gun this way and that and practised lining it up against imaginary targets. He found, slightly to his dismay, that this wasn't so easy. His right eye, although now rid of the bandage, was still almost shut, liberally smeared in Martha's goose-grease and capable of detecting only a pinpoint of light. How long it was going to be before he could see properly with it again was guesswork. Martha reckoned several weeks yet but had expressed her relief that he was not losing the sight of it altogether as she had at first secretly feared.

For the moment, though, that problem did not diminish in any way his joy in handling the gun. It brought him a sense of power that he had never had before and he felt capable of facing up to the Kellys and all their kin whenever they wanted to make a real fight of it.

At the farm, Emma was pleased to see him armed and better able to take care of himself but Martha seemed less enthusiastic and said little. Len practised aiming whenever he had a free moment but found it difficult to line up on a target. He was right-handed and aimed naturally with the right eye but felt that he was not getting it done as he should.

Next morning, he went outside determined to use a very few rounds of his precious ammunition so as to get the feel of the gun. He loaded the Colt slowly and carefully, deriving a peculiar pleasure from inserting each bullet. The gun felt better than ever in his hands and he already had a feeling of proud ownership. Wilson's inititals, JTW, had been engraved into the butt but Len had decided, as soon as he got some money together, to have that tooled out and replaced by his own. The idea of having this gun carrying his name made him feel pretty good.

Old Skin was in the yard, sweeping up, and Len asked him to set up a target. An old bottle was put up on top of a fence-post and then, as an afterthought, Len stepped into the house to warn the women about the shots, just in case they thought they were again under attack from the Kellys. Emma came out to look and stood at the door, arms folded, and with an expression which showed that she was by no means certain what to expect.

Conscious of her gaze, Len took careful aim. He had not, in fact, done much shooting before. A couple of times he had fired off a few practice-rounds from guns borrowed from men at Taylor's place, but that was about all.

His first shot went wide and he pursed his lips in annoyance. He tried again, lining up the target with his left eye but using his right hand, which was all he could do. He missed again and snorted in irritation.

"You ever fired a pistol before?" asked Emma pointedly.

"Yeah, some," he answered shortly.

He aimed once more and then lowered the gun, overcome with uncertainty and inwardly cursing his blind eye.

"When I was young," said Skin suddenly, "I used to go fishing with a spear."

"Thet so?" Len was not interested and found the interruption irksome.

"Yeah. I always missed if I aimed straight at the fish. When I threw the spear a little bit to one side, I nearly always hit it."

"Somethin' to do with the reflection," grunted Len.

"Refraction," supplied Emma.

Len sighed. Emma was swell but sometimes too smart. He aimed once more, lining up with his one open eye, and then shifted a little to the right. He pulled the trigger and the bottle exploded into a thousand pieces.

"Looks like you've shot a fish," commented Emma.

Old Skin reckoned that he had not really interfered in the white troubles by helping the young feller to shoot straight. He had only just been talking about the fishing.

★ ★ ★

All that day was spent with the fence mending. Len and Skin worked constantly at it until near nightfall, when the last stretch of wire had been attached to the last post and they began to gather up the remaining coil of wire and the wood which was left over.

They were just about to carry these burdens back to the shed near the house when a shot rang out from the woods at the other side of the maize-field and a bullet clattered its way through the hanging twigs and foliage of the trees behind them.

Skin dropped to the ground. Len half crouched, gun already out of the holster. He saw, or imagined he saw, a movement in the woods opposite and fired a shot in that direction, less in the hope of making a hit than as a gesture of defiance. He went down on to one knee then, gun still at the ready, head level with the tops of the maize stalks, eye searching, ears alert.

They waited for a long time, expecting at any second to hear the whistle of a bullet overhead or feel the sudden shock of its impact. No further shot was heard, however, and at last they decided to make their way, in a half crouching, cautious walk, around the edge of the field and back towards the house.

As they went, Len wondered what it had meant. Had it been a genuine attempt to kill him or was it intended only as another means of frightening them, another contribution to the campaign of terror aimed at the defenders of the small farm? If it had been the former it seemed unlikely that their assailant would have contented himself with one shot only. A man hidden in the trees on that far side of the field, and armed with a rifle, had an advantage that could not be matched at that distance by the Colt.

Whatever the reason for the shot, it was not repeated. The rest of the evening went by in peace but the incident had a disturbing effect upon them all and they remained in readiness for further trouble.

It came that night when the wood and fields were shrouded in darkness. A light showed at the far end of the maize-field at the wood edge. This fiery light became two and then multiplied and spread. Within moments the tinder-dry crop was well ablaze, the fire rapidly sweeping all across that area of the field and then, pushed on by a rising breeze, beginning to move like a torrent towards the house and outbuildings. Flames shot high into the sky, lighting up the tops of the nearby trees, the vegetable patch and the house itself.

From the start it was apparent that the blaze could not be controlled by a few people armed only with brooms. Nevertheless, Len and Emma ran out towards it, desperate to do something, but were halted by the heat before they could approach. Instead, they found themselves being driven back to the farm buildings where they were immediately occupied in stamping out and smothering the multitude of tiny wisps of fire which floated over on the air and descended upon the roofs of the wooden sheds and the barn.

They worked with an intensity which sprang from the sense that they and the farm were being overwhelmed. Everything around seemed to be drowning in thick smoke and heat. They pounded and stamped and beat at the dozens of tiny fires which sprang up on all sides. They ran through the choking smoke from one point to another as flames threatened to gain a grip and set the sheds blazing. Their hands and arms and faces smarted from a host of tiny sparks, their eyes streamed and lungs choked from the thick acrid smoke which enveloped them. Muscles became rapidly exhausted from the constant labour of swinging and pounding with the hazel brooms.

There could be no thought of pausing even for a moment for rest. The danger was too acute and all were aware of the consequences if they retreated before it. Len and Emma worked feverishly and Martha was there too with her broom, and they became aware that they had been joined by Skin, awakened by the glare and the noise from his shelter in the woods, and labouring now as well as his old limbs would allow.

At last, the shower of sparks began to ease off as the glare from the field subsided. They lifted their heads then to look over what had been a field of ripe maize ready for cutting and saw only a million flickering and glowing points in the darkness, and, nearer at hand, the fence which had separated the maize from the vegetable patch burning itself out. Inwardly, they blessed the green kale and turnips and potatoes and the earth kept moist by their daily chores which had allowed the fire to get no further.

Fortunately, the same wind which had threatened to bring destruction to the farm had borne the flames away from the woods so that a widespread forest fire was averted.

All four stood breathing heavily and clearing their throats while looking over the smouldering stubble. All knew that the loss of their main cash crop was a heavy blow to the finances of the farm, and that there was little chance of recovering from it. Defeat hung in the air with the pungency of the smoke and the ash. All had the same thought but none expressed it. Eventually, Martha sniffed and wiped her eyes with the corner of her apron.

"Well, they've hit us hard," she admitted, "but we're not beaten yet."

"We'll sit here and live on berries and acorns if we have to!" vowed Emma.

There was another prolonged silence, then Len spoke. "Guess I'll go see to the horses in the stable," he said gruffly. "They're all scared with the smell of the burnin'."

He began to make his way towards the muffled sound of neighing and stamping, but had taken only a few steps when he heard the thunder of galloping hooves from the other side of the house and, almost at the same moment, a crash of gunfire and the thud, thud, thud of bullets burying themselves into the wall, the splintering of wooden shutters and the smashing of glass. He ran round the corner of the building, gun in hand, and saw the dark figures of two horsemen careering about while they emptied their pistols at the house.

Anger blazed afresh within him. His Colt came up and he fired, but in his haste and in the violence of his mood the old Pawnee's lesson was forgotten and the bullet went wide. One man turned to face him and fired a shot which struck the corner of the building and sent a shower of splintered stone over his head. They turned then, and rode off into the darkness, two more bullets from the Colt 44 following them as they went.

Len lowered his gun and stood

listening to their hoofbeats receding; then there came a voice floating through the night air. To Len it was the throaty, rough voice of Saul Kelly. The words were indistinct but, as far as he could make out, they were: "Necktie party soon, Finch! Be seeing ya!"

The damage done to the exterior of the house was minimal, but the pain and hurt caused by those bullets which had found their way into the home of Martha and Emma was much greater than a calculation of the actual damage might have suggested. Shutters and panes of glass had been destroyed. Holes had been blasted into the walls of the kitchen and parlour. A mirror had fallen and lay in pieces on the floor. Martha's one fine vase had tumbled from its shelf and lay shattered. A bullet had scored the surface of the parlour table. All this was bad enough, but the real hurt came from the knowledge that the place which they thought of as home had been violated and there was no sense of security remaining. It seemed that the Kellys could invade and destroy as they wished and with impunity.

6

WHEN they came out in the morning, it was to a scene of desolation. What had been a field of maize the day before was now a grey desert of ash, shifting and scurrying in the wind. Charred remnants of broken and gnarled wood were all that now remained of the fence that had marked its boundary. The vegetable patch which had stood as protector to the buildings of the farm had suffered badly in its defence. Row after row of cabbages and potatoes and kale and turnip hung blackened and limp and dead from the intensity of the heat. Those that still lived stood in a landscape of ash.

Somewhat to their surprise, they saw that Skin had come unbidden before sun-up and was already at work, raking the ash into the soil around the vegetables that were unscarred.

"Well," said Martha, smiling thinly, "at least it should make fine fertilizer.

They cleared up as best they could but were interrupted at mid-morning by the unexpected arrival of Holt, Beebo Kelly and two other men whom Len vaguely remembered from the night when the stage had been brought in. They all dismounted without invitation.

"You can jest get back on thet horse and get off our land, Kelly!" shouted Martha, suddenly beside herself with fury.

"Deputy Kelly is on official business, Mrs Benn, as I am." Holt was using his dutiful law-officer's voice. "We're here because of the fire and the shooting."

"You took your time!" Emma was bitter and angry.

"We only heard about it this morning. Cowhand from the Maria Theresa reported that he had seen flames and heard shooting."

"Beebo Kelly could have told you thet, himself, if he had had a mind to!"

snapped Emma, angry and reckless.

"We're here to get at the facts, not to listen to senseless accusations!" replied Holt. "Jest mind what you say, Miss Benn.

"You spoken to his brother, Pete Kelly, yet?" asked Len.

"Pete's been away two, three weeks." Beebo Kelly had a suggestion of a sardonic leer playing around the corners of his thick mouth. "He went up to Jefferson Falls to look for work."

There was a dumbfounded silence, then Martha laughed in a dry, bitter way that Len had never heard from her before.

"Can't imagine any Kelly ridin' half a mile to look for work, never mind to Jefferson Falls!"

"OK. We didn't come here to argue." Holt's patience seemed to be running out. "Let's see the damage done by the shootin'. Nobody hurt anyway?"

"No thanks to the Kellys!"

"Who said it was the Kellys? You got evidence it was them?"

Holt went around the house, noting the bullet-holes, the hoofmarks, the damage done to furnishing and ornaments, then he looked directly at Len.

"You do any shootin', yourself?"

"I fired back at them, sure. What else could I do?"

"See you've got yourself a swell new gun!" Beebo Kelly was grinning broadly. "Where did ya buy thet?"

"Morgan sold it to me. Least, I haven't paid for it yet. He says later will suit him fine." Len was aware that his voice faltered a little as he made the explanation, which suddenly sounded feeble and brought a sense of unease.

"Never knew Morgan to give anybody the time of day without chargin' for it." Holt looked surprised, vaguely suspicious. "Let's see the gun."

"What for? It's all OK. You can ask him."

"Jest my rules, son. Hand it over."

Beebo Kelly had already moved in

and abruptly seized the Colt and pulled it from its holster, warding off Len's protesting hand as he did so. He peered at it quickly but closely before passing it to the sheriff.

"It's got initials on it," he observed in a flat, unconcerned tone which barely concealed a note of triumph. "JTW."

"JTW . . . " Holt examined the letters and turned the gun over in his hands. He seemed scarcely to breathe as he spoke. "Jeremy Thomas Wayne. Colt 44."

"Man called Wilson," objected Len. "Came from Gore Flats."

He suddenly became aware that Holt was staring at him with the look of a fox which has suddenly discovered a rabbit hiding in the grass.

"This gun," hissed the sheriff, "belonged to Jeremy Thomas Wayne, driver of the stagecoach. I've known him for years. There's only one way you could have got this and thet's by stealin' it. You told me you took nothin' from the stage. So you were lyin'. You told me you got thet watch belongin' to Hans Russe from Pete Kelly in a fight but thet must have been a lie too, because he's been away all this time. So you've been lyin' and thievin' and . . . " he paused and licked his lips . . . "it could be thet you've been murderin' too."

"What do you mean?" Martha's voice had a hysterical edge. "This boy's no criminal. I'd swear to God!"

"What do ya really know about him, Martha?" Holt turned to her as if appealing to her to start thinking clearly. "Where did he come from? Out of nowhere! Saddle-tramp! Comes in with news about the stage. Maybe he had a reason for thet. Might have fallen out with the rest of the gang. Thinks he'll cover himself against suspicion, since he has to stay for a while in these parts because if he rides out and meets up with his old pals they'll finish him good. So he pretends to co-operate with the law until he gets a chance to pick up whatever might have been stolen from the stage, thet nobody knows about yet, thet he's managed to stow away some place. Or maybe they didn't find much to steal but he fell out with them anyway about somethin'. Who knows? There's all kinds of possibilities. But one thing certain is thet he's had in his possession this gun and the gold watch, both taken from murder victims. Thet's pretty good evidence for me!" He pulled out his gun and pointed it straight at Len's chest. "You're under arrest. Tie him up, Charlie!"

Before long, Len found himself for the second time in the cell at the sheriff's office in Barker's Fork. This time he knew, though, that Holt wouldn't be coming in the morning with a sarcastic grin and the keys to let him out. He knew himself to be already condemned in the eyes of the sheriff and it was only a matter of time before his trial and execution. The realization was established even more firmly in his mind later that day when Morgan was brought into the office for questioning. He heard their voices raised in animated discussion but could not make out anything of what was said until they came out to the short corridor leading to the front door. At that point he was able to pick up Morgan's parting remarks.

"Believe me, Sheriff, I've never seen that gun before!"

"I believe you." Holt sounded well pleased, self-satisfied. "I knew he was lyin' all the time."

"Terrible thing, them stage murders. Mr Russe too. Thet young feller tryin' to get me mixed up in it! Nothin' to do with me, Mr Holt!"

"I know it! Be seeing you, Morgan. You might have to give evidence at the trial. We'll see."

The outer door slammed. A moment later, Holt appeared at the cell. He stared at Len coldly and then nodded slowly as if all his suspicions had been quite confirmed.

"Looks like you're gettin' to the end of your rope, Finch."

Len said nothing. He was beginning to see the futility of protesting his innocence in the face of the evidence which was piling up against him. Everything he said seemed to brand him once again as a liar and only he knew of the tissue of lies which was spreading all around him like a snare. He knew now what the words of Saul Kelly had meant . . . "Necktie party soon, Finch. Be seein' ya!"

So they had set out to get him and they had succeeded. Anger and bitterness raged within him but he forced himself to remain outwardly calm.

Some time later, Holt and the brawny deputy called Charlie came into the cell and began to interrogate him. He was asked for names and descriptions of the other members of the gang, what had been stolen, what he had hidden and where, where he came from, where his criminal friends came from, had he been in prison, what had he quarrelled with the rest of the gang about, where did he think they would be headed, did he know that if he turned state evidence he might just get a life sentence instead of going to the gallows?

To every question Len answered the simple truth, but it was not to their liking and Holt became more and more angry at what he regarded as the intransigence of his prisoner. Eventually, he stamped back to his office.

"I can't stand listening to any more lies, right now. You stay with it, Charlie."

He had no sooner disappeared than Charlie struck Len in the face, stinging his sore eye.

"Start talkin', yeller-belly, ye're gettin' on Mr Holt's nerves."

A hand slapped Len hard across the cheek. Blinded and maddened, Len jerked forward, hitting out aimlessly. Another blow sent him back on to the cell bunk.

"Hey, what's goin' on?" queried Holt from across the corridor.

"Prisoner's makin' trouble," replied Charlie.

"Yeah, well take it easy."

Questioning and ill-treatment went on for two or three days, at intervals, but Len stuck to the facts until Holt came to the conclusion that he was not going to get any more information out of the prisoner. After that, Charlie stopped pushing Len around and left him to brood long and hard over his situation. Sometimes Beebo Kelly would look in through the bars and grin in that sloppy way of his and make cracks about necktie parties and public hangings. According to him, it was just a matter of time before the circuit judge came around to try the case and after that it would be an easy enough matter to fix up a gallows in the town square so that everybody could get a good view.

Len began to lose count of time in the cell but he reckoned that it might have been about four or five days after his arrest that Kurt Russe came in to the sheriff's office. Len heard him yelling in fury and Holt answering in a lower, more controlled voice. They did not seem to be arguing but Russe seemed to be generally sounding off while Holt lent support by agreeing with him. Before he left, Russe came to the cell and looked in.

"I knew all the time thet you were a murderin' bastard," he growled. "I always had my suspicions of you and I was right. Now you're goin' to get your neck stretched real good. No dirty rattlesnake will kill my brother and live to brag about it."

"You ain't seein' things jest straight, pig-face," replied Len, anger forcing him to a new length of recklessness. "You should be lookin' at the rattlesnakes thet are on your own payroll."

The door was swung open. Two pairs of fists smashed into him. He fell to the floor as a boot thudded into his ribs. He heard them slam the cell shut and make for the street door.

"Circuit judge ought to be here in about three weeks," he heard Holt say.

"We ain't waitin' another three weeks!" ranted Russe. "I'll send for Reynolds over at Creetown. He knows me. Owes me a few favours too. He'll settle thet gopher pretty quick and good riddance!"

The outer door slammed. Holt reappeared and gazed in thoughtfully at Len. There was a hint of unease lingering at the back of his eyes.

"You sure ain't makin' things easy on yourself," he commented drily. "Judge Reynolds will take one look at you and start makin' up the noose himself. He has a real quick way with outlaws — especially when his rich, powerful friends are standing at his elbow," he added, almost as an afterthought, and in a tone which suggested that he was speaking to himself rather than his prisoner.

Kurt Russe mounted up outside

the sheriffs office and headed down the main street. The insult he had received from Len still rankled and he scowled and fumed as he went. He had not ridden far, however, when he saw Emma Benn riding up the street towards him. She was sitting up very straight in the saddle and her eyes were upon him as they drew near to one another. When their horses were about head to head, she drew up and he did the same. He noticed that her eyes were like cold, hard, sky-blue pebbles.

"Russe!" Her voice seemed to have the dry, withering effect of a breeze blowing through the depths of a desert gully. "Martha and me are ready to talk business. I was on my way up to the Maria Theresa to tell you but, since you're here, it saves me gettin' too near the smell of the place. The price is to be what you said before. If it still holds, come around to the farm later today. If you've changed your mind, so be it."

She began to turn her mount around.

Russe held his anger in check. Her contempt cut into his conceit and smarted, along with the remark made by Len Finch, and he had too high an opinion of himself to accept that anyone should ever talk to him in such a way, regardless of how he might have treated them. But revenge could wait until a more suitable time. He had worked hard and long to create the business opportunity which seemed now to be presented to him and he was too astute to permit his personal feelings to get in the way of taking advantage of it.

"Well, if you've seen sense at last," he said, "I'll ride along with you right now. No time like the present.

"I'd sooner crawl on my hands and knees all the way back to the farm than ride alongside you," replied Emma. "Come later on if you want to, and bring somebody with you. You might need a message-boy."

She rode off down the street, leaving him gaping after her. She was approaching the outskirts of the town when she passed the gun store. Morgan was outside, cleaning his windows. Hearing her horse come to a stop, he glanced up at her and then looked quickly away.

"From up here on this horse," said Emma, "I can see right down to the bottom of a prairie-dog hole and there's somethin' away down there thet smells real bad. Do you think you can live with thet for all the rest of your life? Why don't you come out from under thet stone and look at the sun?"

Early that same evening, Russe rode out to the Benn place accompanied by Beebo Kelly and one of the cowhands from the ranch. He had brought them as witnesses to the signing of the document which he carried in his waistcoat pocket. The document was one which he had had his lawyer draw up months before and was basically a bill of sale in which the farm would come to him in exchange for what seemed a generous price. In the same pocket he had the wad of notes with which to settle the deal. He was determined to get the thing done while the Benns were in their present frame of mind. He reckoned that that cuss of a girl could change her mind at a moment's notice and her grandmother probably was no better when it came to this. They had been determined for a long time in their defence of their ownership of the property, so much so that he was surprised now at their sudden collapse, but he supposed that the destruction of their maize crop, the shootings and the arrest of their friend and ally had at last forced them to recognize the hopelessness of their situation.

Other men might have had some admiration for the courage and determination which these two women had shown but Kurt Russe was not like that. Admiration was something which he reserved for himself or for what he saw as a reflection of himself. He was not capable of seeing qualities in others which might be worthy of admiration.

As he drew near to the farm, he cast his eye over its modest buildings and fields and the woodlands round about. The place looked almost worthless but he knew differently and had done so for more than two years past. At that time the railway company, without advertising its intentions, had sent round a couple of surveyors to report on the possibilities of the area in their planned expansion. Russe had not seen these surveyors, and few other people had either, but he knew that when they got back to the city they had presented a report to their employers which was favourable to the scheme. Russe knew that early on, long before anybody else in Barker's Fork had even dreamt of it, because he had a nephew who worked for the railway company. This nephew, Hal Vogel, had no high-flying position — he was, in fact, little more than a clerk — but he had his own ways of taking a look at such documents and was more than willing to pass on information to his Uncle Kurt, so long as he was paid well enough to make the risk worthwhile.

So it was that Kurt Russe knew about the coming of the railroad long before anyone else in the region had heard of it and, in that way too, he knew that the surveyors report had singled out the area around the Benn place as exactly the right spot for the stockyards, railways sidings and buildings required for the development. So it seemed to him that ownership of the farm would enable him to demand a much higher price than the railway company could be expected to pay for other land in the district, and that, coupled with the acres that he already owned, could bring him greatly increased wealth.

However, it all depended upon making certain that these two stubborn women sold the place to him. He guessed that their morale must be pretty low even to consider it and for a moment his ingrained meanness tempted him to try to force the price to a new low, but the memory of Emma's cold stare made him reject the notion. These two women, he felt sure, would compromise no further.

When they got to the farm, Martha came out to the porch and told Beebo Kelly and the cowhand to stay outside while she talked to Russe. Inside the house, she read through the legal document with the utmost care and then passed it to her granddaughter. When they had finished, they nodded quietly to one another before Martha spoke again.

"There are two conditions before we'll sign," she said calmly. "One is that we have two weeks before you take the place over. We need time to get our things together and to move out. Put thet into the paper and sign it."

Russe did so without hesitation. Once the farm was legally his, a couple of weeks with the Benns as rent-free tenants would not matter.

"The other condition is thet Len

166

Finch is freed right now — soon as you can arrange it. We won't sign until we see him free and ridin' out of here."

Russe gaped at her in astonishment.

"What the hell are you talkin' about? Sheriff Holt's got him in custody on murder and robbery charges. I can't interfere with that! He killed my . . . "

"Mind your language in our house! It ain't yours yet, you know, and never will be unless you do as we ask! You've got jest about everybody in your pocket around here, Russe, and I think thet when it comes down to it, Holt will do as you say."

Russe considered. It might just be possible to put enough pressure on Sam Holt but he did not feel at all confident. Holt was still pretty independent and he retained a sense of duty which had not yet been overcome by Russe's money and influence, although he was moving in that direction. He would be very difficult to budge unless some completely new argument or evidence was put before him, but Russe could not think of anything that would be likely to persuade him that he had arrested the wrong man.

"I don't think ya realize your situation here, Martha!" he blustered. "You'll jest starve if you stay on! I don't need to sign this."

"Think you'll jest wait until we starve to death, eh? Thet won't do you any good, as you know well enough."

Russe had, in fact, thought something of the kind more than once. If Martha and the girl both met up with an unfortunate accident maybe he could find a way of getting his hands on the place, but he had given up such ideas since Martha, on one of their previous meetings, had let it be known that she and Emma had already made out a will in favour of their cousins in Sheridan and that these cousins would not sell to anybody but the railway company. No such cousins actually existed in Sheridan or anywhere else, but Martha, although strictly honest in all her other dealings, had no compunction about telling such little lies to Kurt Russe. She was well aware that when you are dealing with a snake you have to use a forked stick.

"You're askin' me to get thet murderer out of jail!"

"The boy is no murderer. I guess you know thet as well as we do."

Russe glared at both of them and then turned on his heel and went outside. He told the cowhand to take a walk while he spoke privately to Beebo Kelly. He outlined the situation to the deputy without telling him any more than was necessary.

"Sam Holt won't buy any of this!" objected Beebo. "Ya know what he's like."

"You could be right there." Russe turned the situation over in his mind once more and then asked, "Who's on duty in the office tonight?"

"Bret Williams."

"OK. I'll tell ya what I want you to do. Get back there, fast as you can, and make some excuse so thet Bret gets out of the place. Jest make somethin' up. Anything. Then let Finch out and tell him to get back here real quick. We'll get Martha to write him out a note so thet he knows it ain't some kind of a trick. Give him your horse. When Bret gets back, make out thet Finch fooled ya into opening the cell door and then knocked ya cold."

"Make out thet I'm some kind of a numbskull, ya mean?"

"It don't matter. You'll be well paid for everything you do to help put this deal through. After it's all over, you can get a posse together and catch up with the bastard and tear his head off, if ya like."

"I'll need to be well paid, I kin tell ya." Beebo Kelly, Russe noticed, was sounding less servile every day and sometimes bordered on insolence. "Seems ta me thet you owe me an' the boys a whole heap of money. We ain't been paid for everythin' we've done for you, by a long way!"

170

"You know what we decided. When this place is signed over to me, you and your brothers will be paid every cent. Then you can move out and start up someplace else. How could we have fellers like Saul an' Pete an' Abe suddenly waltzing around in Barker's Fork with their fists full of money? Holt would get on to thet in no time. He may be gettin' short-sighted in some ways but he ain't blind or stupid."

"OK. So ya want me ta give this goddamn kid my only horse?"

"Only until he gets back here. Then, I guess, Martha will put him on one of hers. If she doesn't, I'll buy you another six horses, believe me! But get goin', Beebo, I ain't spendin' all night chewin' the fat about this."

A few minutes later, Beebo Kelly, armed with a note signed by Martha and Emma, set off through the dusk for Barker's Fork. He was by no means happy about his errand or the plan that Russe had devised. It seemed to him that there were too many things

171

that could go wrong with it and he did not relish the idea of perhaps finding himself set up face to face with Sam Holt.

Sam Holt, he realized, had always been the blue-tailed fly in the honey-jar. A man who was honest, or who thought he ought to try to be honest, could be a real obstruction.

7

WHEN Beebo Kelly rode into Barker's Fork, darkness had fallen and oil lamps had appeared in most of the windows of the town. There was the usual glare of light from the front of O'Hara's saloon and a knot of shadowy figures gathered around, gesticulating and pushing as voices rose in raucous cries, hoots and loud laughter. There was obviously some kind of a fracas in progress, which was not unusual for O'Hara's saloon, where drunks being roughly ejected was almost a nightly occurrence. If he had had less on his mind, Beebo would probably have stopped to investigate, not out of a sense of duty, but because he enjoyed an opportunity to wield the authority which his position as a deputy sheriff gave to him; and a bit of a rough-house could be quite enjoyable when he knew that he had the ultimate whip-hand as few of the local drunks were stupid enough to seriously defy the law, as maintained by Sam Holt and his deputies.

As he drew nearer, he saw that two or three men were fighting on the sidewalk, just outside the swing doors, and his spirits lifted as he recognized Bret Williams, stepping up from the street in order to intervene. Bret had his back turned to him, so Beebo put his heels to his horse and rode by at a brisk trot, anxious not to be seen by his colleague, at least for the time being.

When he reached the sheriff's office, he rode round to the back of the building, dismounted, tied up his horse and went in by the back door, using his official set of keys. Once inside, he walked quickly along the short corridor to check that Bret had locked the front door before going off to deal with the trouble at the saloon. The door was secure and there was no-one in the lighted office, so he felt that he had a few minutes in which to put the plan into operation. How long Bret Williams would take to sort things out with the drunks there was no way of telling, but generally those little problems were settled quickly enough so there was obviously no time to be wasted.

Len Finch looked up in surprise in the dim light of the cell as Beebo appeared with the keys and unlocked the door. Expecting trouble, he rose to his feet, fists clenched.

"I got somethin' to tell ya, Finch, and I only want to say it once." Beebo's voice was low, his tone anxious and impatient. "Get out through thet back door as quickly and as quietly as ya can. Take my horse and ride outa' town by the alley across the way. Try ta keep your face hid so thet ya might not be recognized. You've ta get down to the Benn place as fast as hell."

"What do ya mean? What's all this about?"

"Shut your goddamned mouth! This

is somethin' thet Russe and the Benn women have cooked up between them. Here's this note from Martha, if ya don't believe me. Read it on the way, if ya can see well enough. Now get goin'! This is the only chance you'll get to pull your blasted neck outa' thet noose so don't argue, jest get movin'."

As he spoke, Beebo propelled Len to the back door and pushed him outside. He watched as the puzzled young man mounted up and vanished at increasing speed down the dark alley. Beebo then left the back door slightly ajar and went back inside to make preparations for the deception, but he had barely stepped into the corridor when the key turned in the front door lock and he heard Sam Holt's voice and that of Bret Williams.

Within seconds they were inside and Beebo had time only to slip back around the corner that led to the tiny washroom. In his mind he cursed Kurt Russe and his crazy plans. There was no chance now that he could pretend to have been overcome by the prisoner; no time to mark his face and dishevel his clothes and to lie in a crumpled, barely conscious heap on the floor of the cell. In any case, putting on such an act well enough to convince Sam Holt was a different thing altogether from convincing Bret Williams.

The only possibility now was an opportunity to slip quietly out of the back door and get far enough away to avoid being implicated. He could see, however, that that was not going to be easy as the light from the office still shone across the corridor, showing that the office door was at least half open. He remained quiet, holding his breath and hoping that one of them would draw the door to. Bret Williams seemed to be giving the sheriff an account of the trouble at O'Hara's.

"Jest the usual drunks. Thet feller Leitch, allus makin' trouble. I'm gonna' slam him in the cooler one of these times!"

"Yeah, you're right, Bret." Holt

seemed scarcely interested.

"I told him thet next time there wouldn't be no second chance!"

There was a long pause, broken eventually by Sam Holt.

"What do you think of this town, Bret?"

"Eh, well, what do ya mean?"

"I mean, don't ya think it's beginning to stink, Bret?" Holt's voice had an edge to it that Beebo had never ever heard before. "Can't ya smell the corruption? Can't ya taste it everywhere ya go?"

"I don't rightly know what ya mean, Sam."

There was another long pause. When Holt spoke again, Beebo recognized the edge to his voice as that of a — kind of despair, mixed with desperation and self disgust.

"I'm gonna' give this to ya straight, Bret; at least, as straight as I can. Jest before thet trouble started at O'Hara's, I was walkin' up Primrose Street, jest behind the saloon, and I meets up with Morgan. He looked as if he'd been hit

178

by the yeller fever or somethin'. Like he was ill. But he says he wasn't sick except in his mind. Then he starts to tell me another story about that gun. 'Mr Holt,' he says, 'thet was all lies I was tellin' you. I gave the young feller thet gun, right enough.' Holt's voice lowered suddenly, as if remembering that Len Finch was nearby in the cell and might be awake. "He says, 'Mr Holt, I knew all along thet the gun belonged to Jeremy Wayne because I fixed it for him about a year ago when the safety-catch started to stick. I never saw it, though, from thet time until Saul Kelly brought it in to the store and told me to find a way of passing it off on Finch. He said thet he knew Finch was lookin' to buy a gun and thet Mr Russe wanted him to get this one. The way Kelly spoke, I knew what he meant, Mr Holt, because I owe a lot of money to Russe. He could put me out of business next week if he had a mind to. Now, I've spent all my life building up this business and it still ain't much but it's all thet I've got. I know Kurt Russe can destroy me and I think he will now thet I've told you all this, but to tell ya the truth, Mr Holt, I ain't been able to sleep nights, thinkin' about thet young feller goin' to the gallows because of my lies.'"

The sheriff's voice broke off as if expecting a reaction from Williams.

"Well, goddamn! The lyin' little stoat!"

"Don't blame him, Bret." Holt sounded weary, almost defeated. "We're all liars when you get right down to it, and he's had the guts to come clean at last. But thet ain't all. Jest as he was finished telling me this, up gets this old Injun feller, the old Pawnee, Skin, they call him, from behind a couple of barrels."

"Thet old drunk?"

"Yeah, but he was stone-cold sober, for once. I don't know if he heard what Morgan said or not but he jest looks me in the eyes, like as if he was about ready to call me out, and says, 'Mr Holt, in the old Injun wars there were some helluva Injun fighters among you whites and the only one around here was old Pa Kelly who died years ago. Them old fighters,' he says, 'allus collected in stuff like arrers and tomahawks and shields thet they picked up from their Injun enemies to keep in their old age to remind them about what they'd done.' Then the old feller jest turned around and went off up the alley."

"What in hell did he mean by thet?"

"He means, Holt's tone was steady and measured, "thet the Kellys shot up the stage and used the old man's Injun arrows to make it seem like redskins."

"Nobody was took in by thet Injun rubbish!"

"Nope. Nobody was took in by it and only a damn fool would have thought of it. Some of them Kellys ain't too bright. Thet Saul Kelly, for instance, has no more brains than O'Hara's draught-horse. It's the kind of fool thing thet he could think up!

The worst thing about all this, Bret, is thet I knew it all the time, jest like I've known all the time about the Kellys tryin' to drive Martha Benn off her place. Worse than thet, I knew all along thet the only man who wants thet farm is Kurt Russe, and I should have gone up to the Maria Theresa and told him thet to his face but I never had the guts, Bret, jest like Morgan. Him and me are jest about in the same league when it comes to yeller streaks down the back. I always knew Kurt Russe was behind it but I still let him talk me into takin' on Beebo Kelly as a deputy, even though you know as well as I do thet he makes a lousy lawman. It's only a matter of turnin' round and lookin' at yourself as you really are, instead of seeing yourself with your eyes half shut and squinting. Thet's the way I've been seeing things, Bret, and it's only because I ain't had the guts to face up to Russe because he's rich and powerful and he has friends in high places and he could ruin me jest like thet little rabbit Morgan."

The sheriff's voice trailed off. There was another prolonged silence as if they both stared at each other, waiting for the worst part of the truth to appear.

"What about the stage, Sam?" Bret sounded nervous.

"I'm gonna' do what has to be done about it. It's the most terrible thing. We'll have to go to the Maria Theresa, Bret. We got to shoot at the brain before we clip off the claws. You with me, Bret?"

"I'm with ya, Sam."

These were the last words that Sam Holt and Bret Williams ever uttered. The heavy bullet from Beebo's Colt 45 blasted through the back of Bret's skull and splattered his brains across the ceiling. The next two bullets caved in Holt's chest and threw him across the room and up against the iron stove. His face struck heavily on the metal as he went down and fell as a quivering, bloody corpse in the corner.

For a second Beebo Kelly stared at

the carnage he had created, and then he turned and ran out the back door and around the building. He appeared in the front street just as a small group of people were gathering.

"Hey, I heard shots! What's happening?"

"Seems like it came from in there, deputy. Sheriff's office."

Beebo raced up the steps and into the office. For a moment, he stood in the doorway and viewed again his handiwork, then he ran out into the street once more, his face contorting into an expression of the utmost horror and alarm.

"The sheriff!" he yelled. "Somebody's shot the sheriff!"

The next few days went by with excitement and rumour and speculation running wild in Barker's Fork. What seemed like the most intense activity took place around the sheriff's office. Here, Beebo Kelly stepped in to take over the sheriff's duties in a temporary capacity until such time as he could be officially appointed. For a start, he formed two posses and sent them off to catch up with that low rat Len Finch, who had managed to steal Bret Williams' gun and had used it to murder him and the sheriff. Beebo did not accompany either of the posses as he reckoned that he had more than enough to do co-ordinating things from the office, but he sent them away with strict instructions to do everything humanly possible to bring the criminal to justice. So the posses set off with little idea of where to start looking and led by men like Charlie, who were not noted for their brain-power.

The truth was that riding out on a wild-goose chase was not in any way to Beebo's liking, and he felt that it might be just as well if Finch managed to flee the territory instead of being brought back for trial. It was possible that the young feller's testimony might have a ring of truth about it, especially if he could produce Martha's letter, and added to that was the undoubted fact that Beebo Kelly was not held in anything like the high level of public esteem as had been enjoyed by Sam Holt. A judge and jury might perhaps be just as inclined to believe Martha and Emma, and perhaps even Finch, as they would be likely to accept at face value the word of a Kelly, even if he was, for the time being, acting as sheriff. This suspicion lurked at the back of Beebo's mind and he believed, therefore, that it would be better if the matter were not put to the test. He needed time to establish himself in his new position, which was one that he had no intentions of giving up. He believed that he could hold on to it too, given a little time and the support of Kurt Russe.

So he went through the motions of organizing the search while doing everything he could to mislead and to misdirect. On the second day after the double murder he had a long and private conference with Kurt Russe and on the third day there came to light a ghastly accident in the shape of Morgan the gunsmith, who was found lying on the floor of his own workshop with his neck broken, having, it seemed, fallen from a ladder.

It was while the undertaker was going round to collect Morgan that two men rode in to report to Beebo Kelly. They had been attached to one of the posses but had somehow become separated from it and, not being able to catch up with the main body, had decided just to come home. Both seemed pessimistic about the chances of arresting Len Finch and were not enthusiastic about continuing with the search. Beebo pretended to be annoyed at their attitude but gradually the tension went out of the meeting and they began to converse in a friendlier way. It was then that one of them mentioned, just in passing, that they had seen what looked like Martha Benn's mule-cart, accompanied by two or three horses, moving away down the southern trail. The man mentioned it out of casual interest because it had not been generally known that the Benns were going. Beebo had not known that they were going so soon either, and that day he rode out to the Maria Theresa to inform Kurt Russe.

So it was that Kurt Russe went to take over his new property earlier than he had expected. His mind was full of suspicion and he had a good look around the farm as he rode up to the front door. The place looked empty but there were things lying around outside that he would have thought the family might have wished to take with them. There was a heavy ploughshare, for example, old but still serviceable, and a water-keg that was worth a few dollars.

The front door was unlocked and he pushed it wide and went inside with the growing feeling that all was not as it should be. He observed at once that the Benns had taken little with them. All the larger pieces of furniture remained, the curtains still hung at the windows and there was a rug on the floor. Some ornaments and the picture that had been on the wall were all that seemed to have been removed as far as he could tell at first glance. The deal table with the bullet-score across its polished top still stood in the parlour, the door of which stood open, as if inviting him to enter. It was as if the Benns had left in a hurry, perhaps even on the same night as he had parted from them after the contract had been signed.

Something on the deal table just inside the parlour caught his eye and he went over to the doorway and looked in. There was a letter lying on the polished surface which was kept in place, somewhat incongruously, by a large stone from the yard. Even from the short distance, he recognized at once the bold copperplate handwriting of his nephew, Hal.

Russe did not touch the letter but leaned over it, his tense fingers outstretched on the table top.

"Dear Uncle Kurt," he read, "I am writing to let you know that things are not going as planned. I found out today that, by a majority decision, the Board of Directors has decided not to go ahead with the Barker's Fork development. They feel that because of the way things are going in ranching and farming they would do better to extend much further south in the Powder River region. I thought I should let you know this straight away so that you can take the appropriate action.

"Incidentally, I am enclosing a silver medallion which I came across in a curio shop last week. As you can see, it is Austro-Hungarian, dated 1780, and has a fine portrait of the Empress Maria Theresa. I know it is the kind of thing that is of great interest to you. It cost me five dollars and I would be grateful if you could let me have the money as soon as you can as I have not had a raise in salary for about three years.

Hope you are well.

Your affectionate nephew,
Hal.

P.S. I shall send this by Uncle Hans, who is returning from his visit to the city tomorrow. He is very disappointed too about the railroad but he paid me the five dollars.

Kurt Russe read through the letter three times without moving, though the muscles in his arms and neck grew tense and colour swept through his face. He then turned, leaving the letter where it was, and stalked out of the house. There he stood for a few minutes, breathing hard and swearing out loud. He looked at the run-down, desolate farm which had cost him three times its current market value, and kicked at a length of fencing until it gave way.

After that he rode into Barker's Fork and straight to the sheriff's office. There he found Charlie with his feet up on the table and one of Sam Holt's cheroots in his mouth. Charlie told him that Beebo Kelly had gone home but had left him in charge just in case there were any emergencies, but things were pretty quiet now that the search for the escaped outlaw had been more or less called off.

Russe said nothing but turned and rode back out of town towards the Kelly homestead. On the way the skies darkened and the rain came down in torrents, soaking his clothes and turning the trail into slopping mud and puddles. He did not notice his physical discomfort through the inferno of his thoughts. It was obvious to him that the letter had come from the stage and that Finch had something to do with it, and that the Benn women had left it for him to see so that he would fully realize that they knew that they had fooled him. Otherwise, they could as easily have burnt it in the stove and allowed him to find out much later that the railroad was not coming. It was a gesture intended to rub his nose in the dirt, and that thought burnt in his brain with a greater pain even than the loss of all that money. The thought of the old woman and her granddaughter sniggering at him as they took the trail to the south maddened him beyond endurance and he vowed revenge over and over again as he forced his mount splattering and splashing towards the Kelly place.

It was an undoubted fact that the deal was perfectly legal. The Benn women had taken advantage of information that they had but which he had been unaware of. It was no different than the methods he had employed himself against them and a good many others. The only doubt lay in their possession of his letter, but that had been returned to him. Not that Kurt Russe was any more concerned with legal niceties. The law, to him, had always been something to use when it was to his advantage but otherwise to manipulate and twist and ignore. In any case, now that Sam Holt was out of the way, there was nobody to quote the law to him and no-one to obstruct any of his plans. The law around Barker's Fork had taken on a different shape and that shape was one which he was forming with his own hand.

That fact he intended to take full advantage of and the opportunity had been supplied through Martha and Emma themselves, in their desire to show their utter defiance of him and to offer him insult. The two weeks grace which Martha had negotiated had been intended to delay his finding of the letter until they were well on their way to safety. They knew, too, that he would be certain to look for revenge, but had not been able to resist the temptation to spit in his face on their departure. That part of their plan, however, had not been so successful. He had found out the way things were much earlier than they had bargained for, and the lead they had was not one which could not be rapidly reduced.

Through the veil of falling rain he could just make out in the distance the rough shape of the cabin which was the Kelly family home. Russe had rarely visited it before. It had always seemed to him to be no more than a den of beasts and as such it was a place to be avoided in the same way as he would skirt around horse-dung in the road or keep upwind of a pigsty.

There were times, however, when men like the Kellys were essential to the advancement of Kurt Russe and he had never hesitated to use them when it suited his purposes. Over recent years he had used them more often perhaps than had been wise. He had bought their ruthlessness and their bestiality with promises of money which could not be fully paid out under the vigilance of Sheriff Holt but could not be much longer withheld. As Beebo Kelly had impudently pointed out to him, it amounted now to a considerable sum and he knew himself to be unwilling to pay it.

Also, they knew too much about his affairs because he had not been able to employ them without making them a party to some of his ambitions. The thought that they might attempt to blackmail him had occurred to him more than once but he had always taken comfort in the knowledge that they could not betray him without making a noose for their own necks. Also, a man of his stature in the community would be believed in preference to the Kellys in any court of law. The danger had always been, though, that their stupidity could lead to suspicion against himself in the minds of more intelligent members of the community and investigation might reveal evidence that could not be denied.

For those reasons, Russe badly wanted to rid himself of the Kellys. His plan had been to pay them off on the condition that they left the territory altogether, which they would almost certainly have done since Barker's Fork had never held any future for them so long as Sam Holt held the reins. Things were different now, though, in more ways than one. Beebo Kelly seemed to fancy himself as permanent sheriff and, no doubt, his brothers believed that they would flourish under his protection. That was something to which Kurt Russe had no intention of lending his support. The simple truth was that he regretted using his influence to make Beebo a deputy. At the time, he had thought it would be useful as a counter-measure to the irritating honesty of Sam Holt, but now it represented a danger in the same way as a pack of wolves which produces a powerful leader from within its own ranks becomes a greater menace than ever before. No-one could be safe from their fangs and they no longer distinguished between friend and foe.

A pack of wolves, however, was something that he could make use of in the present circumstances. It was, in fact, the only thing that would serve his purpose. The Benn women must be hunted down and torn to pieces.

He would have his revenge and, he firmly believed, he would be rid of the wolves also.

8

RAIN rattled on the rusting corrugated iron roof of the Kelly household. A broken shutter flapped at a window. The ramshackle porch swayed in the rising breeze. The yard was a sea of mud with an island of horse-dung a little to one side. Four horses were tethered to the fence, their heads lowered in neglect and misery. The fields around played host to a multitude of waist-high weeds. It was a place where the qualities of human decency and industry had long been defeated and only selfishness and indolence held sway.

Russe dismounted carefully and splashed through a puddle to the porch. He stepped high to avoid putting his weight on the rickety boards which served as steps and after the most perfunctory of knocks, pushed open the door and went in.

He caught his breath at the sudden change from the fresh air outside to the thick stench which filled the room. The cloud of tobacco-smoke mixed with that of the stove struck at his lungs. There was a medley of other odours too: stale food and stale sweat, beer and spit, and something else that he could not, at first, put a name to, but which reminded him vaguely of a rotten carcase.

The thickness of the smoke made the room dim so that he had some difficulty at first in seeing. When his vision cleared, he saw that the Kellys were seated at the rough table, playing cards. Tin mugs stood in small pools of spilled beer. Cents and dimes and notes of small denomination were gathered in little piles beside their owners while a larger pile grew in the middle. Somebody had dropped a bowl of soup on the floor and the passage of feet had scattered and trampled it into a stinking mess.

Abe and Saul looked up in surprise at his entrance, pipes drooping from loose mouths. Beebo looked up also but then leaned back with some hint of the conceit and arrogance which had come to him along with his silver badge.

"Well, if it ain't Mr Russe," he drawled as his face split into a grin. "You're just in time to take a hand of poker." He smirked sideways at his brothers. "Maybe give us a chance to win back some of thet back pay ya owe us!"

His brethren snorted into their beer. Abe coughed and spat on the floor. Kurt Russe refused to allow himself to become rattled at the insolence. He smiled as if in appreciation of the joke.

"OK, Beebo, you can count on me for your money. No need to worry on thet score."

"Is thet so, Mr Russe? We was beginnin' to wonder, thet's all. Thet right, fellers?"

Abe and Saul chuckled once more, beards heaving.

"I came to speak to you fellers about somethin'." Russe suddenly found it harder than he had imagined to broach the subject. "Could do with your help."

"Yeah?" Beebo Kelly's grin was pure sarcasm. "Didn't think you'd ever want no help from us, Mr Russe."

They snorted and grunted in their merriment. Abe slapped his thigh as if it was the funniest joke ever. Beebo laughed out loud and then studied his cards as if remembering that he had more important matters to attend to.

"Raise ya two dollars," he challenged, after some thought.

There was much staring at cards and hesitant shuffling of coins and notes. The pile of money grew a little larger.

"Goddamn!" said Saul.

There came a prolonged silence. All seemed deep in thought. Russe kept his temper with difficulty. Taking offence at the bad manners of the Kellys was not in his plans at this time. Abe looked up at him, as if suddenly remembering his presence.

"What was it ya wanted, Mr Russe?"

Kurt Russe swallowed hard. The stink of the place was getting to him and to have to ask for further co-operation from the Kellys in their present mood was like something sticking in his throat. Beebo Kelly, he reckoned, needed to be reduced a little in size.

"Came to talk about a couple of things. Thet star you're wearing, for one thing, Beebo. I'd like to see ya as sheriff but it ain't jest up to me. As a permanent office, it's subject to the election of the citizens of Barker's Fork."

Beebo looked up at him sharply.

"Thought you could fix thet. You got influence. Ya said thet before!"

"Well, yeah, but there's a few other possible candidates. I hear they're likely to get support."

"Tell us who they are and we'll blow

their heads off!" chuckled Saul, slapping Abe playfully across the shoulder.

Russe grinned.

"It ain't thet easy. Wish it was. I'll do what I can to get you elected, Beebo, but I came up to tell ya thet it might not be possible. Don't build up your hopes too high."

Beebo's mouth tightened. He banged on the table with his fist.

"Once a Kelly, always a Kelly, huh?"

"What in hell's wrong with us Kellys?" asked Saul, surprised. "What the hell d'ya mean?"

Kurt Russe shrugged.

"I'll do what I can but I can't promise anythin'."

Beebo's eyes showed unease and disappointment. He had always had the feeling at the back of his mind that it was too good to be true. He could tell by Russe's tone that there was just about no hope of pulling it off and he had a respect for the judgement of Kurt Russe in such matters.

"I'm gonna take it ill out if I ain't

elected," he stated with blunt surliness. "Could be I'll start sayin' the wrong kinds of thing around here, if I get mad."

This was a line that Russe had expected.

"Sure, sure, say what ya like, Beebo, but we're all sittin' on the same horse."

"Some hoss!" yelled Saul, delighted.

"Could be we'll all be swingin' from the same rope!" yelped Abe, anxious to make his contribution to the general jocularity.

"You've got more ta lose than I have," said Beebo, looking Russe straight in the eye.

"I've only got one neck, same as you. Anyhow, what the hell, I didn't come here to argue with ya, Beebo. We're all on the same side. We got to help each other."

There came a deep groan from somewhere behind Russe. He turned round, suddenly scared at the sound which was almost animal-like in its pain and distress. He found himself looking at the door leading to the next room which was slightly ajar. The rotten carcase smell had grown stronger.

"What was thet?" he asked, turning to the Kellys for an explanation.

Abe shrugged.

"Thet's Pete."

"Pete? What do ya mean? What's wrong with him?"

Saul grunted and shuffled his cards. He drank from his tin mug and smacked his lips.

"Pete's not so good. Goddamned bullet-wound's pretty bad. Always hollerin'."

Kurt Russe turned as if to advance to the bedroom and then changed his mind.

"The bullet he took at the Benn place, ya mean?"

"Sure, what else? Only took one bullet, small calibre too, but it's well inta his shoulder. Must be stuck in the bone. Couldn't get it out. Abe, here, worked on it with his knife for long enough but it wouldn't shift."

"Too deep," confirmed Abe. "Couldn't get to it. Stinkin' like hell now!"

"Turned septic," explained Beebo. "Gangrene's set in."

"What about the doctor? You get a doctor?"

"How the hell could we bring in a doctor? He would have reported it to Holt, sure thing, and thet was the last thing ya wanted. Holt would have found out about them raids on the Benns and maybe a lot more as well. Ya didn't want thet, did ya, Russe?"

"What about a doctor now?" Russe was not too concerned but there was something disgusting about the whole thing. It was like somebody had left a mess lying around and he was smelling it and he wanted it removed. "Holt's outa' the way. You could make up somethin'. Huntin' accident or somethin'."

Beebo shrugged helplessly.

"Too late, now, I reckon."

"Reckon so," agreed Saul, spitting.

Kurt Russe nodded in understanding.

He thought, one down, three to go . . . What had he been thinking about?

Something seemed to snap in Beebo. He threw his cards down on to the table.

"What did ya want to see me about, Mr Russe?"

Russe noted the change in tone. Beebo Kelly was irritated, angry and disappointed, but the defiant and aggressive attitude had waned.

"Well, it's like this, Beebo, the Benn women have cheated me. They sold me thet farm only because somebody told them thet the railroad ain't comin' through here at all. They got me to pay far more than the place is worth."

"Is thet so? But the railroad . . . ?"

"It ain't comin'. They were right about thet. There won't be no big changes around Barker's Fork now. Place is all washed up. Not much future here for anybody, if you ask me."

"Ya mean ya was fooled by them two women?" Abe looked amazed and amused.

"I put too much trust in them. Anyhow they ain't gettin' away with it. I'm goin' to get that money back, if you'll help me. I want them caught up with and I want every cent returned to me. If you boys will do thet, I'll make it well worth your while. They ain't got more than about three days of a start. They're on the south trail and they're goin' pretty slow with their mule-cart. You can catch up with them easy, especially when they won't be expecting to be followed so soon."

"What do we get outa' it?" asked Beebo.

"I paid thousands of dollars for thet place. I'm willing to give you fellers one third of it as a reward."

Saul gaped. Abe whistled between his teeth. Beebo looked thoughtful.

"OK," he murmured, "we'll do it."

They decided to waste no time. No preparations were made for the journey except to don hats and coats, lifted from the floor, and to check firearms and ammunition. They were all well-armed with rifles and handguns. Food seemed unimportant to them. There was little in the shack to take with them but, like wolves, they could pick up what they needed on the way.

Russe accompanied them outside to the yard, glad to get out of the stench of the interior. The sky was beginning to clear but rain was still falling. They mounted up, suddenly eager to be off. The prospect of getting their hands on all that money seemed to shine like a star before them.

Beebo hesitated for one moment, looking down with half-closed eyes at Russe.

"You can depend on us. Be seein' ya."

"I know I can, Beebo. I'll be lookin' forward to givin' you thet reward. You deserve it."

They galloped off through the mud, much too fast for the start of such a journey. They were headed by way of Barker's Fork. After a short time, Beebo slowed them down.

"We'll stop at the store for some supplies. We'll get all we need and more."

"You got money?" asked Abe in surprise.

"Who needs money? I'm still sheriff here. We can charge it to the sheriff's office. Goddamned next sheriff can pay for it."

"Thet so? Well, let's get there!"

"And let's get our hands on thet third!" Saul seemed wild with excitement. "Pretty good thet, ain't it? A third of all thet money? Thousands of dollars!"

"Three thirds, thet's what we're gettin'! Ya can count on it!"

"Three thirds! For Christ sake, how much is thet?"

"Enough to set us up for life! So long, Barker's Fork! Damn ya to hell, Kurt Russe! Serves ya right, ya big gas-bag!"

"Yippee! Three thirds! Ya sure about thet, Beebo?"

Back in the mud of the yard, Kurt Russe watched them go. They were far, far out of earshot but he could have paraphrased their conversation with a fair degree of accuracy. He knew they would not come back. That money was too much for the Kellys to bring back to anybody. He had known right from the start that the money was lost to him, ever since he read that letter in Martha's parlour. There was no way of recovering it, but he had determined at that same moment that the Benns would not have it either. They would not live to enjoy it. No old woman and her impudent granddaughter would insult Kurt Russe and live long enough to laugh about it in later years.

He had set the wolves on them and the wolves would tear them to pieces. Beebo Kelly and his brothers would leave nobody alive to witness against them. He could imagine the bullets tearing into Martha and then the torment that the girl would endure before they murdered her also. The thought brought a little smile to his lips. She in particular would regret having insulted him. The cold eyes which had stared their hate of him would fade and die under the brutality which she would suffer.

Also, he was rid of the Kellys. They would take the money and then probably fight and kill one another over it. There would be a new sheriff in Barker's Fork. It would be a man who would owe much to Kurt Russe and would do his bidding, but he would know much less about his master than had Beebo Kelly. He would be no threat and the law would learn to balance its justice to suit Kurt Russe and the Maria Theresa.

The failure of his plans with the railroad was a severe blow but he would recover from it and spread his empire in other directions. There could be no limit to the Maria Theresa as long as he lived.

With that thought in mind, he turned to go to his horse. As he did so, a flash of white caught at the corner of his eye. Startled, he looked sharply over at the porch where a pale, human shape hung on to the creaking timbers, one arm outstretched for support, the other hanging limply, legs almost buckling in their weakness.

With some slight sense of relief, he recognized Pete Kelly. For a second he had imagined something else, something sinister and ghost-like. He smiled to himself at the notion that his nerves must be more shot up than he had thought. There was nothing sinister about Pete Kelly. He made a pathetic figure, hanging there in his unwashed underwear and bare feet, hair and beard a wild mass, eyes half shut and empty of light like those of a dying man.

The smell of the rotten carcase hung in the air, stronger than ever. The stench came from the soiled bandage wrapped roughly around the sick man's shoulder and from the arm that drooped, bloated and blackened like the limb of some slaughtered beast left too long on a butcher's hook.

"Russe." The voice was scarcely audible and seemed to rise up painfully from the depths of tortured lungs. "You saw my brothers ride off, didn't ya?"

"Yeah. They've gone." Russe looked with disgust at Pete Kelly, irritated to find himself delayed by him.

"Won't be back neither."

Russe shrugged. He saw no reason to spare Pete Kelly's feelings by any show of concern or any attempt to pretend that his brothers had not finally deserted him. In a moment he would ride out and leave this talking corpse to lapse into silence.

"Looks like you're on your own."

Pete Kelly's eyes widened just a little. His mouth twisted into a drooling half grin.

"Been on my own fer a long time, Russe. Ever since I was born, jest like the rest of the Kellys. Some family of brothers, heh, Russe?"

Russe grunted his impatience and began to turn, anxious to get away from this stinking man and the stinking place. His movement was only half made when Pete Kelly made a jolting, agonized effort and withdrew his supporting arm from the corner of the porch. He swayed drunkenly, dirty toes spreading out as if to grip the boards, but he now held his free hand steady and Kurt Russe saw that it held a gun and that the gun was small and black and showed part of a pearl handle between Pete's fingers and thumb. The barrel was pointed straight at Russe but the shudder that went through him was not caused by the direct threat but by his recognition of the weapon itself.

"Ya know whose gun this is, Russe?"

Kurt Russe did not move. No words came to his dry lips.

"Belonged to your brother, Hans. Ya kin see thet, cain't ya, Russe? Real swell piece, ain't it? Rich man's gun. Sure ya told us to take nothin' from the stage thet might be evidence but then Saul had to start takin' in the guns. Too much of a temptation fer a Kelly. Ya should have thought about thet, Russe. Ya kin never trust Kellys. So when I sees Saul helpin' himself, I guessed I may as well have Hans Russe's gun and his watch too. After all, it was me thet killed him. Leastways, I pulled the trigger but it was your hate thet did the murder. I shot your brother, Kurt Russe, but it was you thet murdered him."

His voice faded but then returned with renewed strength and with a crazy pitch to it, like that of a man demented by pain and fever. Russe watched carefully, waiting for him to fall, ready at the first opportunity to pull his own gun from under his arm, a fine pistol too, an exact replica of the gun held by Pete Kelly, for they had been bought as a pair, for a pair of brothers, in earlier and maybe happier times.

"Kurt!" The Christian name came as a curse, as if to draw a sharp distinction between Kurt and his brother. "Ya know why ya wanted him killed? Two reasons, Kurt. One was thet ya couldn't ever stand sharin' with anybody, not even yer own brother! You had to have everythin' — swell house, big ranch, power, everythin' to yourself. And the other reason, Kurt, was thet Hans was a good man. Folks respected him for himself and not jest because he was a big-shot rancher. But ya couldn't have thet, could ya, Kurt? Money and power are all thet count with you!" His voice rose to a new height of delirium. "So ya killed yer own brother, Kurt! Thet's about as low as ya kin get! You're as low as the Kellys because there's no brotherly love among the Kellys neither. I been thinkin' about brotherly love a helluva lot all the time thet I been lyin' in thet stinkin' bed, day after day, night after night, full of pain and sufferin', while them brothers of mine were sittin' around, drinkin' and playin' cards and hollerin' and laughin'. It was jest like I was some poor dog layin' there a-dyin' and nobody could take the time to tie a stone around its neck and sling it in the river . . . and now they ride off and leave the dog to die. But thet's Kellys. Thet's the way we've allus been and thet's why you could use us, Kurt, to do all the dirty work thet ya didn't want to mess your hands with. Ya always made use of us in thet way because ya knew we were jest scum thet ya could wipe off your boots when it suited you . . . "

His voice faltered and trailed off. He slumped forward on to his knees. Russe's hand shifted towards his armpit holster but halted as Pete's hand and eye steadied. Instead, Russe spread out his arms as if appealing for reason.

"Hey, Pete, you're real sick. You don't know what you're doin'. Here, I'll help you back to bed and then I'll ride in to town and fetch the doctor.

He'll fix you up. You'll be as right as rain in no time."

Pete Kelly's lips grimaced. For a second a flicker of light came into the dying eyes.

"Too late for me, Kurt. Too late fer you too."

The gun roared. The bullet ripped through Russe's chest and lodged in his lung. The impact threw him backwards, heels slipping in the mud, arms flailing in wild terror as if to fend off the blow that had already struck home. He fell with a dull thud and then twisted and raised himself on to one elbow, knees bent and feet seeking a new grip in preparation for flight, but then the pistol fired for a second time and the blow of a granite club thundered into his skull. Darkness came in a rush and he fell into it, fear perishing on the way.

But his torture was not yet over. Light came back to him, flickering and wild, and he saw again the white figure move against the dark. It was the figure of a dead man, pale and long-haired, and its smell was of corruption. The eyes were dead too but still the figure moved, slowly and stiffly as if from the cold of the grave. He knew that he was looking at a corpse that feebly sought a renewed lease of life and that the corpse was that of his brother, Hans, and that the life was that which he, Kurt, had torn from him. Terror rose to engulf him and he quailed as the spectre raised the gun once again, with a slow, slow movement and took aim at his heart. For a second, the pearl-handled gun held steady and then trembled violently just as the finger tightened on the trigger. Russe turned away his head as if to blot out the fearful sight and the bullet took its erratic course across his face, gouging out the bridge of his nose and searing his eyes.

All was dark, all was numb. There was no pain and no feeling, only the weight of stone upon his forehead and the blackness of the tunnel of death.

Then he heard a voice calling and calling, crying and crying with the piteous wail of a child in distress. And the voice cried over and over again, "Hans, Hans, Hans . . . " and it seemed to Kurt Russe that it was his own voice calling and crying, but he did not know why that should be so since he knew that he cared only for himself and for the things which he had taken from life and which were of use to him.

Then the numbness lifted like mist from the hills and in its place rushed in the fire. His eyes burned like lumps of molten lead, the flames raged through his brain, his nerves twisted in their agony and curled and blackened as grass under the prairie fire. He thrashed and screamed in the hellish torture of it, wildly seeking some means of escape, but the pain hung on to his mind and bored into his skull with its smoking branding-iron and he crumpled under it and groped for darkness and oblivion.

Then the waters rose up all around

him and they had the darkness of earth and the red of blood. They poured in upon him and filled up his lungs and the heavy taste of blood was in his mouth and he knew himself to be drowning. He gasped for air but none came. He heaved and retched and shook but there was no relief from his torment. Only the fire was extinguished and replaced by an agony no less hard to bear, as he drowned in his blood-filled lungs and sank into the depths of the sea of red until the merciful blackness washed over him.

So Kurt Russe lay in the mud of Kelly's yard with his head and chest a bloody mass and his limbs contorted in their last agonies. The rain fell upon him, mixing with the blood from his wounds and that from his lungs. His face lay in the filth and his fingers were thrust into the dirt. His coat had fallen a little open and a pearl-handled pistol glistened wetly and cleanly against the dark mess of his once fine waistcoat.

On the porch, Pete Kelly slumped

forward. The gun fell from his grasp and bounced from the cracked and filthy boards to the pool of rainwater below. Helplessly, he slid after it, head and shoulders slithering into the mud. The rain thrashed with renewed force upon his back, soaking his soiled underwear and the straggling mane of his head and neck.

The rain cooled him a little, calming his fever and clearing his mind. The pain of his corrupting flesh had lessened but he knew that he could not move. There was no strength left in him but he knew that he had a little longer to live, which meant that he had a longer time in which to die.

9

THE rains of the last few days had swept the sky clean and it stretched now taut and blue and pierced only by the hot weight of the sun.

All around, the prairie aroused itself from the downpour, reaching up its stalks and leaves and flowers and shaking off the points of glistening wetness. Prairie dogs scampered amid their burrows and here and there little flocks of finches flew from clump to clump of seed-heavy grass.

The mule-wagon dried out and the beasts pulled well in the morning sunlight before the long heat of the day would bring fatigue and ill-temper. The load was not so heavy but the way was rough and the journey had already been long.

On the buckboard Martha and

Emma were in good spirits, talking and laughing and planning for the future. Ahead of them, in their imaginations, they saw a new farm and a fresh start and with each succeeding day and every mile that fell away behind them, they felt their optimism growing and their sense of elation rising at the thought of the new life which was beckoning them.

A little to one side and slightly to the rear, old Skin rode on an elderly chestnut mare which belonged to the two ladies. Martha had asked him to ride so as to relieve the mules of his weight, and sometimes when the going became hard Emma would mount the black or the roan for the same reason. Skin had not ridden for many years and he now found that he had mixed feelings about it. To start with he had been secretly delighted at the prospect as it brought back to him some of the sense of dignity that he had enjoyed as a horseman in former days and with it memories of those times. On the other hand, he discovered that age had done nothing to improve his seat in the saddle, and his knees and legs and back ached in ways he had never known before. Not that he voiced any complaint or gave any sign of his discomfort. He was too well aware of the honour that had been done to him and would not have marred the brightness of the day or the joyful humour of the ladies by allowing even the faintest grumble or grunt to escape from his lips.

He was, in fact, truly amazed to find himself in their company, and flattered that they had thought to invite him. When he had walked back to the vicinity of the farm from Barker's Fork that night, he had been surprised to find that they had loaded up the wagon with their lighter possessions and were about ready to set out, regardless of the blackness of the night and the difficult trail ahead. Before then, of course, he had known that they intended leaving, but it was a real surprise to him to discover that it was to be so soon.

He had some idea of the reasons for the hasty departure but was a little uncertain as to detail. There was no doubt in his mind that it had something to do with him and with Little Bead Woman. When he had decided to show Martha the little silver picture of Little Bead Woman he had been disappointed to find that she seemed much more interested in the bit of paper with its crazy sign-talk which he had kept to wrap up Little Bead Woman than she was in the silver moon picture itself. She had looked real close at the paper two or three times with a strange expression spreading over her face, and when Emma had looked through the sign-talk she had yelled out like a cowhand and had slapped him across the shoulders in her delight.

After that, he knew that they had had a big talk with Kurt Russe, even though they hated his guts, and had agreed to do what they had always resisted doing, which was to sell him the farm, but no doubt that was because of the fire and the young feller being shoved in jail and all the other troubles which had beset them. Nevertheless, he felt pretty sure that the two ladies had made up their minds to do that only after he had come into their kitchen to show them Little Bead Woman. On the whole, he thought it was a pretty good decision, in spite of the fact that Kurt Russe was getting his own way, because things were sure to be better in the future well away from Barker's Fork and the Maria Theresa.

When Emma had seen him standing in the darkness watching their preparations to be off, she had signalled for him to come over and had then asked him if he would like to go too, and something in her voice had warned him that to stay behind might be unwise. So he had come with them, glad for once to feel wanted by people and glad enough too that he was leaving behind O'Hara's saloon and the whiskey for, since Little

Bead Woman had come to him, he had felt increasingly that he should turn his back on that demon and should go out to meet her.

So now he was riding out over the prairie with the wind in his hair and the feeling that he was somehow moving back in time and was content to do so.

In fact, the least content of that little cavalcade moving over the wide plains on what was generally referred to as the 'southern trail' was Len Finch. He had dropped back a little way from the wagon and rode in silent alertness, his ears tuned to sound behind them, his head twisting at frequent intervals so that he could stare back along the way that they had come.

In his heart there were grave misgivings, and these had been with him ever since the night he had been freed from jail and had ridden back to Martha's place and had there been met by Emma with a fresh horse and some food and instructions to keep out of sight for a few days before catching up with them on the southern trail. He had taken her advice and had kept his head low, riding by way of the woods and the more rugged country until he had of necessity moved out to the open range to meet up with them.

He had ridden with the threat of the hangman's noose about his neck because he had no trust in Beebo Kelly or the word of Kurt Russe. When he had caught up with the wagon and had been told of the letter and the reason for the hasty departure, he had felt it to be a mistake as he saw Kurt Russe as a snake whose instinct must be to strike back. So although he had appreciated the point of the act of bravado and had laughed along with Emma and Martha as they told him of it, he had, at the same time, felt his spirits sink. He had in him now, he knew, that caution and unease which remains with a man who somehow steps aside from the gallows and which takes a very long time to shake off.

So he had got into the habit of riding some distance behind the mule-wagon and keeping all his senses alert. His right eye was still almost closed but he could see well enough with the left and scanned the horizon time after time for the first signs that they were being pursued. Emma was aware of his mood but said nothing. Under her cheerful smile she too had the uneasy feeling that Kurt Russe might not be so easily disposed of, but it was a feeling that she tended to suppress rather than allow it to destroy their present optimism.

Just behind her, on the floor of the wagon, lay the light squirrel-rifle. It was the only firearm they had.

"Where are we about now?" she asked Martha, at noon.

"Shouldn't be too far from the Absarokee river. Then we follow along the east bank until we hit the main trail for Broken Shaft."

"Long ways to go yet?"

"Sure, long ways, but we'll get there. Nothin' to stop us."

In the early afternoon they came to a halt to make coffee, have a light meal and rest the animals.

"Hey, jailbird, make yourself useful and get a little fire goin'. You'll be jest about ready for somethin' to eat, I suppose?"

Len dismounted slowly. In the back of his mind a wolf was raising its head over the grass.

"Think we should?"

"Think we should what?"

"Light the fire. Smoke might be seen from a long way."

Emma looked at him closely, a shadow creeping into her face.

"You seen somethin', Len?"

"Nope, jest a feeling."

"We lit the fire yesterday and before."

"Yeah, I know." He grinned, trying to assume a cheerfulness that he did not feel. "Probably jest my imagination! Been in jail too long. Seen too much of Beebo Kelly and Holt. Still . . . "

"We could jest drink cold water,"

put in Martha. "Save time anyway."

"Yeah, we can do without the coffee until nightfall," said Emma. "No sense in wasting time if we don't have to."

They drank tepid water from the butt in the wagon, ate biscuit and cheese and looked into the sky. Conversation did not come as easily as usual. Len's mood had affected them all. Even the old Pawnee seemed uneasy. He recognized the Kurt Russe feeling. It was like the nightbird, spreading its wings.

A couple of hours later they caught their first glimpse of the Absarokee, a gleam of light in the distance as the waters reflected the afternoon sun. There was the appearance of trees too as clumps along its banks. The sight of it excited and cheered them as it seemed another milestone on their way to a new life, and they stirred the tiring mules into greater effort and beamed at one another, their earlier feelings of anxiety forgotten for the moment.

When they reached its banks, they

halted to refresh the animals and themselves and they took time to stand on the watery boulders and gaze over the broad expanse of tumbling coolness. They had just hitched up the mules once more and were about to resume their journey when the old Pawnee, standing up on a rock by the river, called out a warning that froze their hearts.

"Men on horses comin'. Way back there. Looks like trouble."

They followed his pointing arm. In the far distance there was a little black dot which spread itself out to three and then merged itself once more, only again to separate. Sometimes the dots came to a brief halt as if to study the trail made by the wagon and the horses through the grass before moving on, seeming to grow a little larger even in the few minutes that it took to whip the mules into activity and overcome the inertia of the wagon.

They followed the bank of the river with as much speed as was possible but from the start it was obvious that there was no chance that they could escape being overtaken. When they looked back they could make out the shape of each horseman and saw an arm raised and a rifle held high as if in threat.

Shortly afterwards came the sound of the first rifle-shot. It was still a long way off but the sound filled them with dread.

"That's Kellys!" snapped Martha. "Sure thing."

Emma and Len knew what she meant. Only the Kellys would fire off shots at that distance with no hope of reaching a target and for no reason except maybe to scare their quarry.

As the Kellys drew nearer, of course, their shooting became more dangerous. Bullets flew overhead. One or two splashed into the river, another splintered a stone not far from Len's horse. It was still wild and erratic but it could only be a matter of time before one of the party was hit or an animal brought down. Once as they turned round to look back they saw one of the horsemen draw his mount to a standstill and take more careful aim. The bullet sang close over the roof of the wagon.

"That's Beebo Kelly," said Martha. "Only one with that much sense."

The bank of the broad river had fallen away below them and the current was still swift and the water deep. Away ahead, however, they could make out a line of white and then a stretch where the surface was smoother in appearance. As they drew near, their hopes began to rise as they realized that there might be a ford at that point and a chance to put the river between themselves and the Kellys. It was the hope of a drowning man snatching at straws, because if they could cross by the ford, wagon and all, then it was obvious that they would soon be followed by the Kellys. Nevertheless, they pushed on simply because it was the only line of action which was open to them, and it seemed better than the alternative of being shot down where they were.

When they reached the ford, they were forced to slow to a walk and cajole the unwilling mules into the water. Len dismounted, grabbed hold of the reins of the stubborn beasts and threw his weight into the task. They made a clumsy, splashing, noisy progress, interrupted by frequent stops and wild attempts to turn back the way they had come. At any moment he expected to step into a pothole or have the wheels of the wagon jam between stones. At last, though, they reached the far bank, and there the mules surged forward, anxious to find firm foothold. They pulled the wagon up to slightly higher ground and came to another halt just as a rifle-bullet smacked into the timbers near the rear axle.

"Get them movin'!" yelled Len to Emma as she leapt, wet-skirted, up to the buckboard.

There came a hideous scream from

behind him and he turned to see a wounded horse buck and rear and then tumble down the slope to the boulders below.

"Damn the pigs to hell!" he shouted, almost beside himself in sudden fury which overcame his fear. "Red! Red! Get them horses up and goin'."

The Pawnee led the remaining horses up the bank and then mounted the chestnut with stiff awkwardness. In a moment they were moving forward at a trot and the wagon was gaining a little speed under the furious lashing of Emma's whip.

"Hey, Len!" Martha was leaning out, looking back and calling. "Hurry up! Jump on!"

He realized that in the confusion the Pawnee had led his horse off with the others. He ran after the wagon and had almost reached it when Martha gave a little scream and fell headlong into the grass. As he bent over her, he saw that her arm was covered in blood and the sleeve of her dress ripped. He tore away the remaining cloth and found that a bullet had grazed her forearm and hand. Also she was stunned by the fall and lay quiet and scarcely breathing.

The wound to the arm did not look serious. It was bloody and painful and her arm would be stiff and sore for days but it could not be fatal if it was cleaned and looked after. She should be all right although the scar would be with her for the rest of her life.

The rest of her life? He gazed at her old arm, scrawny and suntanned and toughened by decades of work, and suddenly he felt that the arm was already dead, as it hung limply in his hand. For the first time the utter hopelessness of their position struck him, not just as knowledge in the mind but as a certainty in the soul. Within a very short time Martha would be dead and so would he be, and Red and Emma. The Kelly bullets would rip them apart and their corpses would lie scattered in the grass.

"Len! Len! How is she?" Emma was clambering down from the wagon, her face pale with fright. Her voice galvanized him into action. He picked up the unconscious old woman in his arms and staggered forward.

"Get back on the wagon, Emma, she'll be all right! Don't waste time! Here, take her shoulders."

Between them, they got her on to the buckboard and eased her into a more comfortable position. Emma put a coat under her head and then looked at her arm.

"Emma, dress the wound later. It ain't too bad. She'll be all right for a while. She's comin' round already." He reached past her and picked up the squirrel-rifle. "Give me thet box of ammunition, quick as you can, then get this team on its way, fast!"

She stared up at him, searching for his meaning.

"You can't hit the Kellys from here with that gun. They're still out of range."

"They won't be for long!"

He looked over the top of the wagon and saw the Kellys approaching fast. They were close enough now to be individually recognized. There was Beebo Kelly and Abe and Saul, all of them intent on murder, their narrow minds full of the lust to wound and kill, and it seemed to him that he saw too, in his imagination, Kurt Russe standing behind them, away back at Barker's Fork, with his heart full of murder too, and his fists full of silver dollars to pay for it.

"Emma." He made his voice as steady as he could but they were both aware of a slight tremor. "If we go on the way we're doing, they'll surround us and shoot down the mules and go on shootin' until they've killed all of us too. The only chance thet we've got is if I can keep them back for a spell so thet maybe you can get away to somewhere safe or meet up with some people. The only place I can keep them back at all is right here at this ford."

"I was thinkin' maybe if we mounted up the horses, but now there's Martha . . . " Her voice trailed off in despair.

"There's only three horses left. Somebody would have to stay behind, and Martha can't ride anyway. You have to go on for her sake, Emma, as well as your own."

"You're goin' to let yourself be killed for us?"

"Maybe it won't come to thet." He was aware that he sounded less than convincing. "But unless I can keep them back we're all dead. That's certain, ain't it?"

She stared at him, blue eyes wider than he had ever seen them. Then, to his astonishment, she stretched up and kissed him on the cheek. He snatched up the squirrel-rifle and ammunition and leapt to the ground.

"Keep goin', Emma. You too, Red!"

He heard the mule-wagon rumble forward as he ran down to the river.

A bullet ricocheted off a large boulder

as he looked around wildly for the best place from which to command the ford. The cover did not look too promising as most of the larger stones lay well down near the water's edge where he could be seen from the opposite bank. To lie in the grass further up might make him difficult to see but he would have no protection from bullets at all. The only possibility seemed to be a little outcrop of stone about halfway down and to one side which was partly shielded by a straggly bush.

He ran towards it, crouching as he went, and threw himself flat on the ground. He squirmed under the overhanging twigs. There, he worked his body as low as he could make it and slid the narrow barrel of the rifle between the rocks. Hastily, he made certain that it was fully loaded. To his dismay, he saw that the chamber could hold only two cartridges at a time so that, if they decided to make a rush of it, he would have no chance. He must try to hit them before they entered the water and reload with lightning speed so as to get in another two bullets as they attempted to cross.

Even at that, he recognized the fact that his chances of making a good fight of it against their superior rifles were just about nil. The most he could hope for was to wound one of them with his first shot so that they would be discouraged from attempting the crossing, and then lie where he was and hope that he would not be killed or wounded at once by the hail of bullets that must inevitably follow.

He lay as still as he could but knew that his hands were trembling. He gasped for breath and he could feel his heart thumping against the earth beneath him. Desperately he tried to get his nerves under control, but the fear of death was in him and it gripped his mind as it does that of a small animal which lies in hiding and watches the approach of a predator. The waiting was almost unbearable. Gone was the fierce anger which had dispelled his fear a few minutes before. Hatred for the Kellys still consumed him but now it was the hatred which is born from fear itself and as such it was a wavering emotion, ready to give way and to cringe at the feet of his enemies in the hope that they might spare him. In his heart, he cursed himself for his stupidity for having given himself up to death when he might have mounted a horse and ridden for his own life, regardless of the lives of others. Then he thought of Emma's eyes as he had last looked into them and he felt ashamed at the craven ideas which had suddenly gripped his mind. How could he think of saving himself and leaving his friends to die? He thought of Red and Martha and Emma, and then he thought only of Emma and he found that only by thinking of her could he control his trembling body and fearful mind.

Gradually the trembling fit went from him and he pushed fear a little way to the back row of his thoughts.

He tried hard to concentrate on his present situation and how to prolong the coming fight so that Emma might have the maximum opportunity to reach safety. His thoughts did not take him beyond the simple plan which he had already devised but the repetition of it in his mind helped his self-control and he knew that he was calmer than he had been and would do what was best in the circumstances.

There was no sound except the rushing of the river across its pebbly bed. It was apparent that the Kellys had lost sight of him but knew that he was somewhere around and were now approaching with a caution which they had not previously shown.

At last, after what seemed an age, they came slowly into view. The first sight he had of them was a black hat moving over the grass of the opposite bank and then the head and shoulders of Beebo Kelly. He was followed by Saul, both still on horseback but moving at a slow walk. Both carried their rifles at the ready and their eyes ranged from side to side, scanning the west bank of the river for a clue as to his whereabouts.

He remained perfectly still, hoping to make himself invisible. In fact, only the narrow, brown barrel of his rifle was in view and from a distance it merged well enough with the low branches which hung over him. As he peered through the thin screen of leaves, he saw Abe also come into his line of vision, a little further downstream but equally on the alert.

All three stopped and listened and watched, while Len lay prone, hardly daring to breathe. He knew discovery was inevitable but he wanted it to be at the moment when he got in the first shot and not before.

There was a long hesitation. Beebo's head moved and stared, moved and stared, like that of a suspicious antelope at a water-hole. Len guessed that he was beginning to wonder if there was anyone hiding there at all. Maybe they had made a mistake and the Finch feller had crawled away through the grass and was now in pursuit of the wagon, having decided that the odds against him were too great and he had better try to save his own skin while he had the chance.

Whatever thoughts went through Beebo Kelly's mind, he could not remain there all day in such speculation. The wagon and the money were drawing further away and he was impatient to catch up with it. It was necessary to push on, even at the risk of one of the Kellys taking a bullet.

Beebo made a slight gesture with his left hand. Saul nodded and urged his horse down the slope to the water. As he did so, both Beebo and Abe raised their rifles and pointed them over the stream, ready to fire at the first sign of movement.

Len waited until Saul had spurred his reluctant mount a few yards forward into the stream, and then he steadied his rifle as best he could against the rock and took careful aim. His right eye was scarcely open and still almost blind. It all had to be done with his left and it was made doubly difficult by the twisted position he had been forced to lie in. He aimed at Saul's chest and then shifted the muzzle so that it looked to him as if he would hit the man's left shoulder. With that degree of compensation, he hoped to strike the heart or somewhere near it. He was surprised to notice how calm he felt now that the action had begun. Fear still lurked within him but the butt of the rifle seemed to weigh upon it and to keep it in check.

When he felt quite sure that the moment had come, he expelled his breath and softly squeezed the trigger. The shot rang out and the bullet sang past Saul Kelly and struck a branch of a low tree a little way behind Beebo. A piece of bark whipped out into the air. Beebo's horse jerked nervously to one side. His attention was taken up for a second so that he failed to observe where the shot had come from. Abe, however, had noted the spot and fired at the clump of leaves just as Saul, cursing and panicky, pulled roughly at the reins and retreated back the way he had come.

Abe's heavy bullet splintered a stone just a few inches from Len's head. Instinctively, he flattened his face into the earth and then raised himself by the slightest degree and fired again after Saul, this time taking no time to aim. The light bullet nicked the fleeing man's elbow, so that he yelped with pain as blood splattered across his jacket.

Then it was as if all hell had been let loose. The heavy rifles thundered and smoked. Bullet after bullet after bullet struck and splintered off the rocks beside Len's prone figure or buried themselves in the earth of the bank above his head. Twigs rattled and cracked, leaves fell down upon him. He lay as flat as he could on the ground, willing himself to sink into it. Every nerve was as taut as a clock spring as he tensed in expectation of the savage impact of lead, the shrill tearing of flesh and muscle, the crunch of breaking bone. Somehow it did not happen. They were firing from a little below him or on a level, and the rocks shielded his body with no more than inches to spare.

After a time the furious fusillade came to a halt. There followed minutes of silence and then he heard Abe's voice shouting to his brothers above the rushing of the river.

"Did we hit him? I think maybe we got him!"

"Could be!" Saul sounded hurt, blazing with pain and fury. "Hope we've smashed the bastard to smithereens!"

Len turned as cautiously as he could without raising his body and loaded two more shells into the rifle under cover of his low parapet of stone. He guessed that if they thought he was dead or wounded they would come over now in a rush just to make sure.

When they did that, he would have no chance beyond the possibility of hitting one of them, but then he would be dead and the remaining Kellys would catch up with Emma and kill her. So far, they had not attempted to attack in a body because they had not reached such a point of impatience or desperation as to take the serious risk of taking a bullet. The unintelligent venture of Saul had been prompted by Beebo, who, at the time, had not been quite certain that the danger existed and was willing to risk his brother in a situation that he might have balked at himself. Now things were different. A minute or two before, he had been alive and shooting; now he might be dead or disabled but they were not sure. They would wait for a little longer and then attempt the rush, once they had got themselves into the right state of mind.

He knew now that he did not want to wait for that charge. Once they started it, they might not turn back even if one of their number fell, and then he would be overwhelmed and Emma would die. Up to now, the stones had protected him from their bullets. The longer he kept them shooting from the other side, the more time the wagon would have to reach safety.

He peered out again from between the leaves and saw that they had dismounted and crouched almost hidden in the grass of the ridge opposite, rifles still pointing. After a long wait, he saw Abe rise carefully to his feet and mount up. His two brothers began to do the same. Len aimed as steadily as possible, trying to learn from his recent experience. The range was just about right for the light-calibre gun. He pulled the trigger just as Abe began to ride down the slope and saw the horse buck and rear as the bullet ploughed into its neck. In a second it was down and Abe lay struggling in the grass. Even in that moment of crisis, Len felt a pang of regret to find that he had put a bullet into the dumb, innocent animal, but it was an emotion that competed with a sense of satisfaction as he realized that the loss of the horse must impede their progress.

Lead hammered around him once again. He crouched low, as before, until it eased off a little. When he looked out, he saw that he was under fire from two points only. Abe and Saul were keeping him pinned down. Beebo had moved off downstream on horseback. As he went, his eyes never left the surface of the water. He was searching for another way across.

10

LEN twisted his head and watched Beebo Kelly ride along the far bank and then vanish round a bend in the river. There was no way of knowing whether there was another crossing-place further along but it was not unlikely. It happened often that when a river became shallow enough at one point to form a ford, another stretch of a similar depth might be found within a short distance. Beebo might cross within a few hundred yards, or half a mile, or a mile. There was no telling, and the first knowledge Len would have of it would be when he was fired upon from overhead, and that would be the final moment of his life.

There was nothing he could do about it except stay where he was and fight on. To attempt a defensive posture against a possible rear-attack from Beebo could only be done if he exposed his back to the other two rifles across the stream. So far he had stayed alive only because of the low stones which lay in front of him; to move was to die. He would, of course, die soon enough anyway. He lived on only in the hope of taking one of the Kellys with him and prolonging the fight for as long as he could.

With extreme caution, he turned his rifle-barrel a little to the right. He could just make out Abe Kelly's hat amid the grass. He waited and then saw Abe move his head and shoulder. A second later and a bullet glanced off a stone nearby and sang into the bank above. At that moment, Len pulled the trigger and Abe let out a howl of anguish and disappeared.

A surge of triumph ran through him. If he had put one Kelly out of action, then that was something, though not enough in itself. He waited and then felt his spirits sink as he glimpsed Abe crawling through the vegetation, holding the side of his head. Whatever the wound was, it was not too serious, painful but not disabling.

In his imagination, Len saw Beebo Kelly cross the river and ride around behind him. The intense fear which hung on to the back of his mind began again to stretch out its fingers. He knew himself to be afraid of this fear because it could grip his soul as a snake does a small bird and crush all the fight and life out of him. He thought, Emma, Emma, Emma, and turned his rifle towards the black smudge in the grass which was all he could make out of Saul Kelly.

In that second, Saul's rifle fired. The light squirrel-gun leapt like a wild thing in Len's hand as the heavy bullet struck the muzzle. The stock thudded into his jaw, his fingers jarred and stung and let go. The weapon fell from him and rattled down over the stones and pebbles.

For a brief moment, he felt stunned by the blow and then, as his head cleared, he became filled with horror as he realized that the rifle had slid well down the slope, leaving him completely defenceless.

There was only one thing to do and Len did it. He jumped up from his hiding-place and scrambled after the gun, hoping that by some wild chance he might retrieve it and get back without being shot down. It seemed, even at that moment, crazy and reckless but it was better than lying behind the stones to await his execution.

A bullet whistled past his head. A stone dislodged itself beneath his boot. Earth gave way and he slid and fell heavily on to his back. He pushed himself up and bounded forward. Then his heel slipped and his foot went between two stones while his body fell. He felt something go in his ankle. He tumbled to his knees in the wet boulders of the water's edge.

"We got him!" Saul yelled like a banshee in triumph. "We got him now, Abe! Let him have it, Abe!"

"I'll do it my way!" Abe seemed almost overwhelmed with delight. "He's had it comin' and here it comes!"

They came over in a frenzied, splashing gallop, Saul in the saddle, Abe holding onto a stirrup. As they drew near, Len saw that Abe's ear hung in two tattered parts and the side of his face and his shoulder were covered in blood. His expression was that of a mad beast and he swung his rawhide whip savagely in his free hand.

Within a few seconds they had crossed and Len struggled to his feet just as the first whiplash cut across his head. He put up his hands for protection and felt his knuckles split and burst.

"Thet's it! Whip him to death, Abe! Cut him to ribbons!"

Len could see it coming. He could withstand few more of these white-hot lashes before sinking to the ground to die an agonizing death under the savage madness of Abe Kelly, whose lust to inflict pain had reached new heights under the goading of his wound. Desperately, despairingly, he launched himself at his assailant. His bleeding hands grasped at Abe's collar, his full weight pushed into him. Feet slipped on the slimy river bottom and they were both down under the water, struggling for life.

Lungs strained to bursting point. Fingers sought a killing grip at the throat and tore at eyes and ears. Legs and arms twisted in desperate python movements. Sometimes a limb would find leverage and push up a gasping, staring, dripping head for a brief moment above the surface before being dragged under once again. They twisted and rolled and wrestled and punched and Abe bit Len on the arm and had his tattered ear wrenched so that it spread anew its blood through the water.

As the struggle went on, Saul sat on his restless horse in the shallows, his Colt 45 at the ready, hoping to get in a shot at Finch. Time after time he raised and lowered the gun as the combatants splashed and slithered. He badly wanted to put a bullet into Finch but it seemed to him that he could hardly attempt it without putting Abe's life in danger. A couple of times, in fact, his finger whitened on the trigger only to ease off when he realized that he was aiming at his brother's back and not that of his enemy. So he dithered and hesitated and muttered, "Goddamn, goddamn', half under his breath and pulled without thought at the reins so that his horse became more and more disturbed.

After watching the combat for some minutes, however, Saul found that a little demon which had been lurking in the back of his mind for some time was beginning to make itself heard. It suggested to him that if his brother did not come up out of the water then there would be more money left for Beebo and himself. Beebo had said that they would be getting three thirds between the three of them so it seemed to him that if there were only two left to share in it, then they ought to come off better. To what extent, he could not work out, but one thing he was sure of was that two folks sharing a blueberry pie always ended up better fed than three.

So Saul found himself keeping his gun ready for use only if and when Finch emerged from the river, leaving Abe on the bottom. Even when he was given an excellent chance of blowing out Finch's brains and putting an end to the fight there and then, he did not take it. He felt inclined to let matters take their course and it did not look as if he would have much longer to wait because Abe seemed to be getting the worst of it and had not put his head up for some time. He would then kill Finch and explain things to Beebo when they met up.

Thinking of Beebo, he turned round in the saddle in the half expectation that Beebo might have found a crossing and be riding up towards them. The dark figure of his younger brother was not in sight but he saw something else instead — a little patch of grey which moved slowly through the grass on the crest of the river bank behind him.

For a moment Saul could not think what it was, but then by staring hard and squinting under the brim of his hat he realized that he was looking at a head of grey hair with a swarthy face beneath it. It was, without doubt, an Indian, but what would an Indian be doing there, at this time, watching what was going on?

With some sense of alarm rising inside him, Saul turned away from the river and urged his horse up the steep bank towards the figure in the grass. As he drew nearer he recognized the old drunken Indian who was always hanging about at the rear of O'Hara's saloon and the realization brought a sense of relief coupled with irritation and annoyance. What the old goat was doing away out here Saul had no idea, but there was no way that he was going to be allowed to spy on him and Abe going about their business.

The old Pawnee rose to his feet as the horseman approached and then fell back as two heavy slugs from the Colt 45 thundered into his chest.

Still troubled by curiosity, Saul gazed down into the coppery, lined features. He was surprised to see that the old man looked almost peaceful, for in Saul's experience most people who are shot to death look quite the opposite. Then the dark eyes opened and there was a light in them that Saul could not understand for they seemed to radiate peace and joy and almost a kind of gratitude, as if Saul had presented him with a bottle of whiskey instead of two lumps of lead. At the same time, the gnarled fingers crawled over the blood-soaked shirt and drew out from beneath it an object that caught the late afternoon sun, and it was round and gleaming, like a silver dollar.

At that, Saul's eyes also lit up but it was with the avarice which was an essential part of his nature. He slipped from the saddle then and reached out to take the silver dollar, but the old Indian's fingers tightened on it and moved as if to keep it safe. Scowling, Saul grabbed the stringy wrist and began to twist so that the hand would release its hold. It was then that the dark eyes opened wider and the calm light in them was replaced by fire, and the old man pushed himself up from the ground and at the same time pulled a large knife from his belt of the kind used for skinning cattle or buffalo.

Saul took the first savage stab in the throat and the blood spurted across the grass. The next blow penetrated his lung and the knife continued to rise and fall, over and over, flashing and flashing in the light until it was too bloody to flash any more, and the arm that wielded it fell back in exhaustion.

Then Saul Kelly lay twisted in death, cut and hacked and disfigured so that even his best friends could hardly have recognized him, if he had ever had any.

Len found them both after he had clambered up the slope, wringing wet, bleeding from his cuts, limping on his twisted foot, and with his fingers still seared along their inner surfaces from the tough leather whip which he had used to strangle Abe Kelly. At least, he thought he had strangled Abe Kelly. Maybe he had just held him under long enough to drown him. He was not sure, for the struggle had been confused and wild and desperate, but it did not seem to matter either way. He was alive and Abe Kelly was dead and he was glad of it, for he had not yet had the time or the leisure to regret the necessity.

When he saw Saul lying dead and old Red dying nearby, he was overcome with a mixture of amazement and grief. He realized that by killing Saul the old Indian had saved his life for he had known all through the terrible struggle in the river that a bullet awaited him. When he had emerged and discovered that Saul had gone he could not believe his good luck or understand what had happened. Now he knew, but he did not know what to think or what to feel because it is impossible to watch a friend die and believe that it must be worthwhile.

He bent over the old Pawnee and put a hand on his shoulder. He was surprised to see the eyelids flicker and half-open. The lips turned up a little at the edges as if to smile.

"Young feller." The voice was hardly more than a croak and scarcely audible. "I brought your horse. Over there, other side of the ridge. Took it away by mistake. Watch out for Beebo Kelly. Remember the spear fishin'."

Len straightened up as if stung. It was a terrible thing to leave the old man to die alone but there was no time for such a consideration. Emma and Martha were still in terrible danger. If Beebo Kelly had crossed the river, as seemed likely, then he might be on their trail right now. The fact that he had not returned to the ford suggested that he had found another way over and the length of time that had elapsed with no sight of him could mean that he had decided that he had more important matters to attend to than helping his brothers finish off Len Finch.

Len picked up Saul Kelly's Colt 45 and then took his rifle from his saddle-boot. Saul's horse looked jaded and half starved and, after taking the weapons and some ammunition, Len turned it loose. He then stumbled over the low grassy ridge and sure enough, just as old Red had indicated, his horse was tethered to a bush a little way out of sight of the river.

Redwing heard him gallop away and after that there was silence, except for the faint rustling of the grass. Darkness was closing in on him, or so it seemed, but he felt sure that he could see, away out there in the dark, the night stars that were the campfires of the ancestors. In his hands, he could still feel the firmness of the silver moon picture and he reflected that he had done pretty well in keeping out of the white folks' wars because he had only just returned the young feller's horse to him, as was only right, and as for killing Saul Kelly, well that had been more of a personal thing, to do with Little Bead Woman and himself . . . and she seemed to agree, and made her voice whisper through the murmurings of the grass, that all was well.

The trail of broken and bent grass left by the passage of the mule-wagon was easy to follow and Len forced his horse on at as great a speed as common sense would allow. His physical and mental exhaustion after the death struggle he had come through was such as to make him feel that he could fall from the saddle, but he forced himself to keep wide awake and to keep going.

Ahead of him the land stretched in a series of undulations until it met the western sky, where the sun of the late afternoon was beginning to spread pink. Away over to his left, he could still see the tops of a wavering line of trees which marked the progress of the river. It was in that direction that his attention was more often focused for it was from there that he expected to see the dark form of Beebo Kelly, taking up his murderous trail.

As he rode, he was plagued by self-doubt but not by fear. He felt uncertain as to whether his tired, bruised and injured body could carry on much further. He did not know if he could catch up with Beebo Kelly or put up a fight against him. Beebo was an experienced killer, quick with a gun and ruthless. He was a formidable opponent and Len had no high opinion of his own marksmanship even at the best of times. Blind in one eye, as he was, and almost exhausted by his recent trials, he had no confidence that he could come out on top in a face-to-face confrontation.

He knew, however, that that was

the way it must be. He had to try to stop Beebo Kelly, and killing him was the only way. If it turned out, as seemed likely, that he, himself, was the one marked out for death, then he could not avoid it. To turn away, to back down, would be to leave Martha and Emma to their evil fate and that he could not do. That was the unthinkable. He knew now that he could not live with the knowledge of such a betrayal and such cowardice, and that fact reduced his fear. Also he had in him now the feeling that death for himself by means of a bullet was not so terrible. He had faced worse, much worse, in that animal conflict in the river.

On the horizon, the pink spread and deepened. There came a gleam and a shadow and then a shape, indistinct and shifting, but he knew that it must be the mule-wagon and his heart leapt. How far ahead it was he could not be sure. The rolling landscape and the changing light made such a judgement difficult. He estimated a few miles only. Not too hard to overtake before nightfall.

If it was easy for him, though, then it was easy for Beebo Kelly. He searched again towards the river and felt a jolt of dismay as he saw a moving shape there too, nearer by far than the wagon, and moving at an angle as if to cross its trail some way ahead.

At the sight, he spurred his mount to greater efforts, for this conflict must come soon and he wanted it to be here, miles away from Emma, so that she could not see him die.

For some time he remained uncertain as to whether Beebo Kelly had seen him or not. Beebo's direction did not waver for a moment and he rode at speed as if the wagon held all his attention. Only once did he hesitate and that seemed to be at the point where he came across the direct line of the wagon-trail through the grass. There, he turned his back fully upon Len and seemed to draw ahead. To judge by his speed he was well mounted, and it seemed likely that he would overtake the wagon before Len had any chance of catching up with him. Len knew that his own horse was tiring and must soon slow down.

It was obvious that the fight had to start soon or it would be too late. Len drew Saul's Colt 45 from his belt and, knowing he was still well out of range, fired it in the air.

The small, partly silhouetted figure ahead suddenly halted. The pale suggestion of a face turned towards him. There was no further immediate movement and Len guessed that Beebo was, at first, uncertain who was following him. It might, after all, have been one of his brothers. After some minutes, however, during which Len continued to advance, he seemed to decide to get on with the business in hand and turned again to take up the trail.

At that, Len's spirits sank. His desire to dive headlong into this death-struggle was paramount and all thoughts of personal safety had gone from him. All he wanted to do was to get to grips with his enemy and have the matter settled once and for all.

To his chagrin, his horse was now showing considerable signs of fatigue. Len knew that he had already ridden it too hard and it must slow down or drop. The pace became slower and with it his hopes of saving Emma seemed to fall away with every faltering hoofbeat.

Overcome with dismay, he drooped his head almost into his horse's mane. His sense of failure swept through him like a flood and the thought of Emma at the hands of such a butcher brought hot tears to his eyes and contorted his face with grief. The world swayed around him and only his habitual horsemanship kept him in the saddle for he desired now only oblivion from an existence which could not be borne.

Minutes later, he looked up and realized that his mount had continued on its way but at a slow pace. To his astonishment, he saw that Beebo Kelly was no longer riding hell for leather for the wagon. He had stopped on the trail ahead, his face turned towards his pursuer, his rifle at the ready.

So Beebo had decided now to settle the threat from behind before going on to deal with the two women. The wagon and money could wait a little longer while he shot down this persistent kid who dogged his trail like a coyote.

Len forced his horse into a trot and went on steadily, his eye never leaving his enemy's face. He knew that he had to get nearer before he could have any chance of using his rifle successfully. The first shot would come his way. It could easily be the last. He must grip his nerves to carry out the only plan that had come into his mind.

The range was still almost at the limit for accuracy but Beebo was a little impatient. Len watched as the rifle was raised to his shoulder; then he counted, one, two, three, four, as aim was taken, and then shivered as the bullet sang past his head. He trotted on, never varying his pace. Beebo lowered his rifle and sat with it on his knee while he watched his approach. Beebo looked relaxed and easy, like a man at a turkey-shoot.

The range rapidly shortened. It was now such that a good shot could hardly miss. But Len was slower than Beebo. He needed time to aim, time to steady himself, time to compensate for that crazy eye. He kept his nerve and came on. He saw again the rifle raised and, at that, he slipped his feet from the stirrups. He counted as Beebo took aim, one, two, three, and toppled sideways from the saddle, letting out a shout of pain as he went. He hit the turf and rolled over as his horse felt the bullet pass over its ears. The sound of the shot and sudden disturbance caused the animal to plunge wildly and to caper off to one side.

For a full minute Len lay still. He guessed that Beebo would be looking for him to get up again, injured no doubt, but needing another bullet. Some men, he knew, would have ridden back to make certain, but Beebo wanted to get on his way. The wagon was still on the move and night was not far off. Quite probably Beebo would not ride back to check the effect of his shot. His conceit in his own marksmanship might see to that. Also, he was a Kelly, and the Kellys were disinclined to tidy up on detail.

With the utmost caution, Len raised himself just far enough to peer through the stalks of grass. To his relief, he observed that Beebo was turning away and putting spurs to his horse. At that, Len stood up, steadied his rifle against his shoulder and took the most careful aim of his life. To fail now was to die for certain. He aimed to the right of Beebo, drawing upon all his recent experience in overcoming his partial blindness, and resisted the temptation to pull the trigger too soon at the receding target. He fired one, two, three, four times, moving the barrel in closer at every shot. He fired until the magazine was empty. Which bullet struck home, he had no idea, but Beebo suddenly jerked in the saddle and fell to the ground.

Rapidly, Len got to his horse and mounted up. As he rode, he pulled out the Colt and held it ready. When he reached the spot where Beebo had fallen his finger was already whitening on the trigger. Then he saw that there was no need. Beebo lay spread-eagled in the grass, his eyes closed, and with a gaping wound in the back of his head.

Relief swept through his mind like a fresh breeze. His spirits soared and the tension of his features broke into a grin of triumph. He had killed Beebo Kelly! He had saved Emma! Beautiful, wonderful Emma! He felt that he could sing out and scream and yell in his sudden relief and happiness.

Beebo, however, was not quite dead, though sinking fast. His breathing could still be heard and now and again he would give a little jerk in hand or arm. The swarthy face looked somehow paler. His thick lips had parted and his tongue seemed to have become clamped between his teeth.

Len gazed at him as he died and his sense of elation fell away. No decent man can crow over a dying enemy, for by that time triumph, blame, argument and self-justification are all too late, because the dying man has entered upon another kind of negotiation which the man who stands over him with a smoking gun in his hand has yet to learn about. He has lost interest in all that went before and the triumphant man with the gun knows that all too well, and is silenced by it.

Len returned Saul's gun to his belt, looked away into the sky and then again at the prone form lying at his feet. So, he had killed two men that day. There was no pride in the knowledge. It left an emptiness in his soul which he believed might take a lot of filling. Not that he felt regret at the deaths of these evil and dangerous men. Reason told him that there could not have been any other way, but the realization of what he had been forced to do brought no sense of victory now, only a feeling that he had done something unclean and the marks could never be really scrubbed out.

So he sat there in the saddle, looking down at Beebo Kelly, and cursed through the tears that sprang to his eyes, and because it is always easier to curse the living than the dead, he damned Kurt Russe to hell, not knowing that he was too late in that also.

After a time, he lifted Saul Kelly's guns to throw them into the grass but then he remembered that there was a long journey ahead yet and who knew what dangers it might hold for Emma and Martha and himself, so he changed his mind, and brought the guns with him. Even so, he knew that there would come a time when he would buy a good clean gun for himself, untouched by any Kelly, and he would use it when he had to and not before.

He turned then and continued on his way towards the red of the setting sun. Tomorrow they would find their route back towards the new life they had planned.

Pretty soon, he made out the shape of the wagon in the distance. It was like a little square shape. After a while, he could make out more detail. Emma was standing up on top, as high up as she could get, as if she were on tiptoe, and she was waving and waving, beckoning him to hurry.

THE END

TOP HAND
Wade Everett

The Broken T was big. But no ranch is big enough to let a man hide from himself.

GUN WOLVES OF LOBO BASIN
Lee Floren

The Feud was a blood debt. When Smoke Talbot found the outlaws who gunned down his folks he aimed to nail their hide to the barn door.

SHOTGUN SHARKEY
Marshall Grover

The westbound coach carrying the indomitable Larry and Stretch headed for a shooting showdown.